TOO FAR TO SEA

Books By Lorin Grace

American Homespun Series

Waking Lucy
Remembering Anna
Reforming Elizabeth
Healing Sarah

Bradford Brides

Rescuing the Sheriff's Heart
Bending the Blacksmith's Heart
Converting the Preacher's Heart
Healing the Doctor's Heart

Heirs & Heroes

The Viscount's List
The Colonist's Petition (coming)
The Gentleman's Agreement (coming)
The Duke's Directive (coming)
The Captain's Letter (coming)
The Earl's Inheritance (coming)

Stand Alone Titles

A Little Clean Fun
Love in the Valley

Artists & Billionaires

Mending Fences
Mending Christmas
Mending Walls
Mending Images
Mending Words
Mending Hearts

Hastings Security

Not the Bodyguard's Baby
Not the Bodyguard's Widow
Not the Bodyguard's Boss
Not the Bodyguard's Princess
Not the Bodyguard's Bride
Not the Bodyguard's Angel

Hastings Legacy

Too Much in Common
Too Far to Sea

Misadventures in Love

Miss Guided
Miss Oriented

Spellbound in Hawthorne

(with Maria Hoagland)
Taste of Memory
Sprinkle of Snow
Hint of Charm
Dash of Destiny
Stir of Wind
Essence of Gravity

TOO FAR TO SEA

HASTINGS LEGACY #2

LORIN GRACE

CURRANT
CREEK PRESS

Blood Donors Everywhere

one

THERE WERE A THOUSAND BETTER ways to use PTO than nursing a sprained ankle. Especially two days before starting vacation. Fortunately, Hastings Security gave compensation time for work-related injuries regardless of how silly the cause.

Abandoning her crutches, Dana stumbled and toppled onto the couch. She pressed an ice pack against her swollen ankle and winced.

Across the small living area of her apartment, her TV displayed a message from the streaming provider asking if she was still watching. It must not be used to her having the service on more than an hour. In the five hours since returning from the emergency room she'd watched more television than she'd seen in months, outside of children's shows that is.

Her stomach rumbled, reminding her she hadn't eaten since the end of school picnic at the park with her young charges. Which app should she order from tonight?

The doorbell buzzed. Who could be here? She glanced down at her clothes, a Hastings Security t-shirt and a pair of basketball shorts, not exactly ready for company. She pulled up the Two Garden Tower app and saw Brit and Simone standing outside her door with a take-out bag from her favorite Italian restaurant.

Dana tapped the option on the app that unlocked the door. "Come on in."

"How are you feeling? Tian said you sprained your ankle playing soccer with the kids." Brit set a box marked "cannoli" on the coffee table.

"I thought Tian was flying to Boston. How did she know?" As soon as she asked the question, the obvious answer came. Tian's husband Chris had been working the protection detail with her. "Never mind. The newlywed news network strikes again."

"I think they have a way to communicate faster than a phone." Simone held up the other takeout box. "The manicotti is warm. Do you want it now or in the fridge?"

"Now please." Dana took the box, napkin, and bamboo fork from Simone.

Simone sat down at the other end of the couch. "What are you watching?"

"Nothing very interesting."

"We could watch *Persuasion*. Maybe it would give you inspiration to find your own Captain Wentworth on your cruise." Brit scrolled through the viewing options.

"*Persuasion* is a second chance love story. Is there anyone in your past you are pining for?" asked Simone.

"Not even a kindergarten crush. And absolutely no one from the last four years. Either guys want to challenge me to wrestle them because I am a bodyguard or they think I am an uneducated airhead because I am a nanny."

"There is always Javier," said Simone with a wink. The head of building security had refined the art of flirting as if it were an Olympic sport.

"Not dating a coworker." Dana slid the fork around the takeout box, gathering every last bit of cheese from the manicotti.

"I think you should have a vacation romance. Cruise ship plus Ireland, that adds up to a Love Boat connection. There could be some cute purser or there's always the best man."

Dana held up a finger. "One, cruise ship employees aren't supposed to date passengers. Two, I've met my sister's fiancé. Wealthy, snooty, and rude, and I assume the groomsmen are all the same."

"You shouldn't make assumptions," said Brit.

Dana rolled her eyes. "As the *half-sister* of the bride, I won't have time to myself. Plus, once Motherzilla-of-the-Bride sees this—" Dana pointed to her foot, "—she'll exclude me from everything she hasn't already. No chance to flirt if I wanted to."

Simone opened the cannoli bag. "We got two for you and one for each of us. Your mom can be the worst."

"Please don't call her my 'mom.' Mom is a term of endearment. I've grown out of calling her my 'Momster,' so please use Sheila, mostly because she hates her first name. Or if you must, you can call her my mother in the most biological sense." Dana so rarely mentioned her mother that she doubted either friend even knew her name.

"Have you told Cheyanne about the crutches yet?" asked Brit.

"She is so stressed. Between the wedding and moving to London and dealing with the Motherzilla, I'm trying to avoid the conversation until she can see I'm alright. The doctor said I should only have to stay off of my foot for the next three or four days. I'll be fine by the end of the cruise and the wedding."

"They'll figure it out when you are in a wheelchair at the airport," said Simone.

"No wheelchair." Her sister would think her helpless and if a photo ever got back to her co-workers, she would never live it down. As it was, the teasing texts over the work app were multiplying. Somehow, ZoElle added a whack-a-mole image that randomly popped up on the conversation channel.

Brit shook her head. "I know you are a tough Hastings Security bodyguard, I mean personal protector, but O'Hare and crutches are not a good mix. Do you have an aisle seat?"

Before Dana could respond, a knock came at the door leading to the Ogilvie's residence. Brit hopped up to answer it.

Chris Johnson, another bodyguard, entered with the largest ice cream sundae Dana had ever seen outside of a restaurant. "The kids made this themselves. They wanted to bring it over, but their mom wouldn't let them."

Three little faces appeared in the doorway. Knowing they would have jumped on her couch and Porter or Peter would have hit her unbooted ankle, she was thankful for Candace Ogilvie's foresight.

The youngest boy leaned into the room. "It's a smiley face!"

"To make you feel better!" shouted Porter the oldest of the Ogilvie's adopted children.

"It was my idea!" Polly pulled Peter back into the penthouse proper.

Chris set the bowl on the coffee table. Dana got a better look. The children topped Vanilla ice cream with two chocolate chips stuck in the center of marshmallow made eyes, a bright red cherry nose, and a long-sliced banana for the mouth. A copious amount of chocolate syrup and rainbow-colored sprinkles on top of the Sundae made up the hair under a whipping cream hat. "Thanks kiddos. This is a perfect dessert to help me heal."

"You're welcome Miss Dana. Get well soon!" Her little charges ran off.

Dana looked from the bowl to Chris. "Can you stay and help me with this?"

"Sorry, no." He swiped the cherry nose. "Someone has to do your job. Ogilives are going out as soon as Mrs. Ogilive puts the kids to bed. I am on duty."

Dana dipped a spoon in the hat. "Good luck keeping them in bed if they ate too much ice cream."

"They didn't." Chris closed the door behind him.

"Grab a spoon, ladies. Before this melts. Cannoli can wait."

"I found your flight reservation." Brit stared at her phone and held up a finger. "Why are you in economy? The amount of flying you've done this year with Hastings I thought you would have enough points to upgrade."

"I'm going to ignore the fact that you can look up a passenger's reservation from your phone." Dana ate a large bite, hoping the ice cream headache would dull the pain in her foot.

"Most employees can't. I'm piloting a new Legacy Airlines app. Perk of being a founder's grandchild. Why the nasty seat?"

"Motherzilla asked me to donate my miles so the bride can fly business." Anything for her sister. Despite the rift with their mother, they had grown close since Cheyanne started college.

"Looks like Sheila and your stepfather are in business, too." Brit rolled through the phone. "I hate to tell you this. They made a block of reservations. You are the only one in economy."

Dana closed her eyes and exhaled slowly. She knew better than to trust her mother with her reservation. "I was told I was sitting with the rest of the bridal party."

Brit bit her lip. "I have some good news and some bad."

"I'll take the bad first." Chocolate dripped onto Dana's shirt. It was a bad news sort of day anyway.

"Bad. On your return flight, business and first class is full, but I can move you to premium so extra legroom. Good news. For your flight there, I have an open first-class seat and I can change you to it."

"Is that ethical?" asked Dana.

"Was it right for Sheila and your stepdad to take your miles for your half-sister and put you in the worst seat in the plane?" asked Brit. "What is the point of having friends who work at Legacy if they can't help you out? Besides, first-class seats make into a bed so you can keep your foot up. Your own private area."

"Another reason to use a wheelchair. You'll be on the plane first. Motherzilla will have no idea you got a better seat." Simone dipped her spoon into the smile.

Brit tapped on her phone again. "There, your wheelchair request is in and your new seat assigned."

Simone held up her phone. "Oh, and look at that. Your favorite flight attendant just traded her Paris flight for London. I promise you will have the best flight."

Dana laughed. "I can't believe you two. Well, if I am getting kicked out of the wedding party, at least I can do it in style."

"If they do kick you out, you should go to Bath and see all the fun Jane Austen stuff." Brit dug into the melting ice cream.

"Or go to Lyme Regis and walk the Cobb. So romantic." Simone ate a marshmallow eye.

"I don't think it will come to that." Cheyanne would want her to stay even if she was in a wheelchair. Her mother didn't want her there to begin with, but Chey would win.

"With all the stuff Sheila has done the last few months…" Brit shook her head. "I thought our family was messed up, but your mother has elevated pettiness to a new level."

The ice cream or her friends were working, at least on her mood if nothing else. And bonus, she wasn't thinking of how she'd injured herself when none of her principals were in danger. "Worst case, I will have to go explore Bath. Maybe I'll find my Mr. Darcy."

"Captain Wentworth is better. Just look at those eyes." Brit fanned herself over the actor coming on the television screen.

Dana studied the man. It wasn't his eyes. It was his almost smile. No wonder Louisa Musgrove jumped off the Cobb into his arms. If only he wasn't fictional.

Two

THE PALE LIGHT OF THE rising moon reflected off the calm waters. McKay leaned against the upper deck railing of the cruise ship, enjoying his favorite time of night. The pools and hot tubs were closed until sunrise. Most passengers had taken to the bars, casinos, or rooms. Lights flickered along the departing coastline, stretching into the distance. Tomorrow would be the final at sea day before reaching the port of Southampton. His radio crackled to life, jerking him from his reverie.

McKay tensed, waiting for the call that would send him running to break up a fight or deal with an over-indulged passenger. The radio sputtered again and fell silent. Even after five years working ship security, he never quite got used to the way trouble could shatter these peaceful moments.

As Deputy Security Officer, he wasn't on duty for the night shift, but as long as he was in uniform in a public area, he kept his radio on.

McKay's phone buzzed in his pocket, and he pulled it out to see his sister's name flashing on the screen. Most nights Jen called so her daughter Gracie could say good night to her uncle McKay. With no one around, he answered the call. He felt the corners of his mouth lift into a smile.

"How are my favorite ladies?" he asked, holding the phone out so they could get a clear view of his face.

"Uncle Mac! Guess what?" Gracie bounced up and down, moving the phone with her. The boundless energy overflowed through the screen.

McKay couldn't help but chuckle at her enthusiasm. "What?"

"I get to go to Robyn's Place this summer. The doctor said my new heart is a good ticker." Gracie's eyes sparkled with anticipation as she shared every detail about the theme park. "I get to be a princess for two whole days. I get a special dress and everything!"

McKay's chest tightened at the mention of her heart. Two years ago, they'd nearly lost her. Now here she was, planning theme park adventures like any other child.

"Wow. That is the new indoor theme park near you, right?" Like everyone in northern Indiana, he'd read dozens of articles about the new park built by billionaire tech mogul Colin Ogilvie's wife for children with special medical needs.

"No, it is far away. We have to drive a long time. Longer than going to school." Above all else, Gracie hated being strapped in a car seat even for a short fifteen-minute ride. The new park was only seventy miles away.

"But it is still in Indiana, which is close."

"You only say that because you are on the other side of the world." Behind her thick glasses, Gracie rolled her eyes.

Jen chimed in. "See how dark it is there? It is time for Uncle Mac to go to bed and we have swimming class in the morning."

"But I am too excited." Gracie's lower lip jutted out, signaling the onset of a tough night for his sister.

Jen widened her eyes and mouthed, "S.O.S."

"Then you need to listen to the special music playlist I sent you. I listen to it on the ship when I can't sleep."

"Can I mom?"

McKay knew what his sister would answer. He'd teamed up

with her during his last visit home to make Uncle Mac's special music playlist full of quiet instrumentals.

Jen turned Gracie in her lap to make eye contact. "If you hurry and brush your teeth."

A mischievous grin spread across Gracie's face. "Deal!" She blew him a quick kiss before disappearing off screen.

Jen leaned closer to the camera, a mix of gratitude and exhaustion evident in her eyes. "Thanks. I thought she'd never go to bed tonight. The invitation from Robyn's Place came in a huge envelope today. I've had the email for weeks. I already received permission and have the days off. They put a countdown calendar in it so she won't have to ask me every day how much longer until she goes."

"I'm so glad you can go. I wish I could be there." Once, McKay doubted his niece would live long enough to go on any vacation. The new Robyn's Place, built especially for children with special medical needs by childhood cancer survivor Candace Ogilvie, was an answer to prayer. The best part is it didn't cost his sister a single penny.

"I wish you could be here, too. I know you have three months on this contract left. We will take lots of videos."

"I'll be home for Gracie and Mom's birthday, as well as Halloween, this year." He didn't mention his next contract would begin before Christmas.

"You better. We miss you." Jen's voice softened. "And so does Mom. She hasn't been herself lately."

McKay's brow creased. "What's going on? Is everything okay?"

"I'm sure it's nothing serious," Jen said quickly. "She just seems tired. She had a doctor appointment today to go over her PET scan. You know how she is about her cancer checkups. Wouldn't let me drive her, but had the Uber here an hour early."

McKay nodded. His mother had beaten cancer once before. Doctor appointments made her nervous. "I'll call her as soon as we hang up."

"Thanks. Love you." Jen waved.

McKay ended the call and stared out at the sea. Worry gnawed at his thoughts.

A couple with arms wrapped around each other walked along the deck, slowing to kiss every few steps. McKay watched them long enough to determine that neither seemed incapacitated before exiting the deck through the nearest crew door and making his way below.

As an officer, he had a small but private room, so he never had to worry about what a roommate might be doing like most of the crew did. While his mother didn't need hearing aids, the background noise of the sea and wind made it difficult for her to hear, and he preferred the privacy of his room for the conversations potentially discussing her health.

Mom picked up on the second ring. She uncharacteristically left her video off.

McKay forced a smile, knowing his mother could still see him. "Hey mom. How are you?"

There was a pause, and then she whispered. "The cancer's back."

The words hit with the force of a tsunami. He sank down heavily into his desk chair. "What? No, that can't be right. There must be some mistake—"

"No mistake," she said gently. "He thinks with chemo, I might have another year."

So little time. McKay struggled too keep his voice even. "When do you start?"

"I need a few more tests. You know how doctors are. Probably in a couple of weeks."

"What is the prognosis if you don't do chemo?"

"Before Christmas."

Less than six months. The realization hit McKay like a punch to the gut. He would be at sea half of that time.

"I wish it were different, but we knew this was a possibility." A quiet strength resonated in her voice.

Struggling to hold back his emotions, McKay asked, "Does Jen know?"

"Not yet. I'm not sure how to tell her. Gracie's summer activities and her job are pushing her to her limit."

"Let me talk to the cruise line and see what I can work out. I'm coming home as soon as I can."

"Don't you dare break your contract." His mother's voice held a resolve missing earlier in the conversation. "Not until I know my options."

"What if I ask about my options? I am two-thirds of the way through this contract. And I've been with them for five years. I am sure I can work something out."

"It is summer, you know it is busy season."

"This is only a job. You are more important." Tears welled up in McKay's eyes. He had experienced the pain of being away from his family when his father passed, unable to get home in time. He refused to let history repeat itself. He would be there for his mother.

Three

THE FLIGHT ATTENDANT CLEARED DANA'S dinner tray. Brit and Simone had been correct about the flight. It had been worth the embarrassment of being pushed in a wheelchair to get on board. She'd only seen her mother for a few minutes, long enough to reassure her she'd be off the crutches before the wedding. During their video call yesterday, Cheyanne had been more amused than upset by Dana's need for crutches. Losing a soccer game to a three-year-old and a gopher hole was funny, almost… The stuffed prairie dog left anonymously, with building security's help, was cute. It would be a long time before she lived her accident down.

"Here is your ice bag." The flight attendant handed her one on a tray.

"How did you know?"

"Simone told me to treat you like royalty." He winked.

"What is her area?" Dana transferred the ice from the plastic bag into the leak proof silicone ice bag she'd brought.

"Main cabin." A commotion on the other side of the dividing curtain caught the attendant's attention as someone tried to pull the curtain aside.

"Where is she? Is she on this flight? I've been back to the main cabin. She isn't there." Sheila's voice rang through the plane. "She's on crutches! How can you lose a woman on crutches?"

Someone answered her mother in a firm voice. "Ma'am, I'm sure she's on the plane. Please take your seat and—-"

The attendant standing next to Dana looked at her.

"My mother, sorry." Dana moved to stand.

He motioned for her to stay sitting. "Simone warned me. I'll take care of this."

Dana sank back into her seat, a familiar mix of embarrassment and anger churning in her stomach. Even on a transatlantic flight, her mother made a scene.

He walked to the curtain separating business and first class. Dana turned to watch the drama unfold, grateful that at least this time she had witnesses to her mother's behavior.

"Do you know where my daughter is? She is supposed to be in the main cabin and there is a strange man in her seat."

"Did you see her get on the plane?" asked the attendant.

"Yes, she was in a wheelchair. She's tall and—" Sheila squeaked as she looked past the flight attendant and her eyes connected with Dana's. "What are you doing here? Why is she in first class?"

Sheila tried to elbow her way past the flight attendant. If there was any karma in the world, someone would record this to post on social media. But that would hurt Chey, so hopefully not.

"Ma'am, please sit down." He blocked the way and pulled the curtain closed.

Dana covered her mouth. The flight attendant had intended to have her mother see her.

"But my daughter—"

"Has a ticket for that seat. You, however, don't have a ticket that allows you in this section of the plane."

"She should trade seats with me. I am her mother!"

"Ma'am, if you don't sit down, I'll ask the air marshal to restrain you and we can land at the nearest airport and deplane you."

"Mom, will you sit down?" Cheyanne's voice was firm. "This is my wedding. Don't you dare ruin it."

A moment later, the flight attendant returned. "Would you like a drink?"

"Actually, yes," Dana answered wryly. "A large glass of patience, with a dash of ginger ale, please."

The rest of the flight passed peacefully. Thanks to the lay flat bed and the television, Dana even slept. However, she couldn't fully relax, knowing her next confrontation with her mother was unavoidable.

The moment Dana hobbled off the plane and onto the gangway on her crutches, her body sagged.

Sheila stood behind the wheelchair attendant with a tight-lipped smile and paper cruise luggage tags in hand. "I told your sister weeks ago we should have excluded you. But she wouldn't have it. However, she agreed to let Chandler's cousin stay in the suite with the rest of the bridal party. You now have an interior cabin all to yourself. Don't miss the bus to the ship."

"Thank you so much for your concern, Sheila." *Motherzilla.* Dana forced a polite smile as she took the luggage tags. She knew better than to let her anger show. She'd play her mother's game for now, but she wasn't about to let this ruin her time on the cruise or her friendship with Chey, which had blossomed while her younger sister attended Northwestern.

Shelia rushed away.

"Do you need anything else, Miss?" asked the attendant, gesturing to Dana's crutches and backpack.

"No, thank you."

"Then let's get you to customs. And don't worry about missing the bus. We get to take the short way." The woman pushing the chair stopped by an electric vehicle which resembled a glass enclosed golf cart. She opened the door for Dana. "I need to find another traveler who needs assistance. Then we'll be on our way."

A few minutes later, the woman returned with an older gentleman dressed exactly like what Dana pictured an old Cambridge professor would wear, down to the bow tie and tweed jacket.

The attendant slid in the driver's seat and turned to Dana. "Where are you going on your cruise?"

"We are sailing around Ireland, then back to London for my half-sister's wedding."

"Well then, let's not miss that cruise bus." The driver circumvented the long customs line and drove the little cart through a designated assistance lane.

When she was the first to reach the bus, Dana tipped the assistant extra, glad that she'd picked up a few pounds while in the states. She wasn't sure that tips were necessary in the UK, but she would rather be generous when possible. "Thank you so much for your help."

Dana watched Sheila, her step-father, sister and the rest of the bridal party herd their suitcases to the bus only to be told they were supposed to drop them with the porter as Dana had upon leaving customs. There were advantages to needing wheelchair assistance. She should have tipped her helper double for showing her the drop off.

At the docks, another wheelchair waited for her, allowing her to bypass the long line of passengers waiting to board and get her key card. Deck 8-1269. Sheila must have planned this room change weeks ago. She couldn't have orchestrated this from the plane.

Using another shortcut, the crew member wheeled Dana onto the ship. A uniformed officer stood at the security checkpoint, scanning cards. Two bars on his shoulder boards indicated his seniority. His bearing spoke of military experience—Navy, maybe. She'd seen enough former military in private security to recognize the telltale signs. But it wasn't his uniform, though it fit him perfectly, that caught her attention. It was the almost-smile playing at the corners of his mouth, as if he found something quietly amusing but was too professional to show it. Her heart did an unexpected flutter when his gaze met hers. *Get it together, Dana. He's just doing his job.*

He stopped her chair. "Ms. Knight? I don't have you listed for wheelchair assistance."

Her eyes met his—a warm hazel that seemed to see right through her. He wore the perfectly non-committal expression most bodyguards used. It was difficult to guess if he would smile or frown next. Dana forced herself to maintain her composure. "Um. No. I just sprained it two days ago. I should be fine on my crutches."

"How?"

"How what? Did I hurt it? Or how am I going to get around this enormous ship," Dana glanced at his name badge, "Officer Worth?"

His neutral expression slipped into a genuine smile that transformed his entire face. "Both?"

"Playing soccer with a three-year-old. And I'll just skip my upper body workouts for the next few days." Dana used her crutches to help her balance as she got out of the wheelchair and slung her backpack over her shoulder. She turned to the young man who had pushed it. "Thank you so much for your help. I'll be good from here."

Officer Worth nodded at her. "Don't forget to check in at your muster station." His voice held a note of concern that seemed more personal than professional. More likely, it was her imagination or the extra ibuprofen.

"Thank you, have a great day." Dana kept her voice steady, though she felt his eyes on her as she maneuvered past the elevators to have her card scanned at the muster station.

Her brief bubble of satisfaction at handling that interaction professionally popped when she made her way to her stateroom. As she expected from her key card number, instead of the spacious multi-bedroom suite her sister had booked months ago, a dark, cramped interior room awaited her. The cruise line had decorated the room trying to counter the feeling, but another light or two would have helped more.

On the bright side, being alone, she wouldn't feel like the crusty camp counselor when the rest of the bridesmaids got seasick or drank too much. Any refund for the difference between her portion of the classy suite and the compact room would go into Sheila's pocket.

Dana sat on the end of the single twin sized bed and elevated her throbbing ankle. The tiny room was small enough she wouldn't need her crutches to hop around, as long as the seas were calm. For her current situation, this was the better option of a room. Something she wouldn't tell her mother. Luxury was overrated.

A glance at the ship's app told her that the closest open food venue likely to have ice was four floors up, near the pool. The others wouldn't open until the ship left the dock hours from now. With a sigh, she maneuvered to her feet and grabbed the crutches, bracing herself for the trek to the upper decks.

Despite her best efforts to focus on navigating the ship's layout, her mind kept drifting back to Officer Worth's smile. She'd met plenty of attractive men in her line of work—why did this one make her pulse quicken? Maybe it was just the pain medication making her light-headed. Yes, that had to be it. Because developing feelings for a crew member would be the worst possible complication to an already complicated trip.

Notwithstanding her bravado earlier, getting around the ship on crutches was daunting. Once at the pool deck, she found she had to cross to the other side. Cheyanne and her friends sat around the main pool already in swimming suits, although it was a cool day. Her half-sister waved her over with a flourish of her mimosa. "Dana! Come join us. We were just talking about going to the casino tonight. You must come."

"Thanks, but I think I'll pass this time." Dana eyed the bridesmaids, who were already tipsy if Lindie's and Erin's giggling was any sign. Renee said something to Amy-Kate behind her hand. The inside cabin was a bigger blessing than she thought it could be. "I should stay off my foot as much as possible."

"It's my bachelorette cruise. Celebrate with me." Cheyanne's gaze slid past Dana, lighting up as she caught sight of a man approaching. "Chandler!"

Dana pivoted on her crutches. Chandler strode towards them, clad in khakis and a polo shirt, looking every bit the proper British gentleman on a holiday. Two of his grooms-minions followed him. His cold eyes raked over her with a hint of disdain. The minions, full on sneered.

"A pleasure to see you again," he said, though his tone indicated otherwise. He turned to Chey. "Sunscreen? I'd hate for you to ruin the photographs."

"Of course. Do you need some?" Chey plucked a bottle out of her bag.

Chandler sniffed. "Remind me to get you some of my brand."

The minions squeezed in between the bridesmaids only after Chandler sat on the end of Chey's lounge chair.

The conversation turned to the sail away party. Dana left as soon as she felt she could. At the outdoor bistro, she asked for her icepack to be filled and treated herself to a warm cookie, which was easier to hold than the celebratory ice cream cone alternative.

Back in her cabin, she propped her foot on the bed with the extra pillow and let the ice do its work. Intending to read her new novel about a viscount and his list of marriageable debutantes, she pulled out her phone. A notification from the Hastings Security app filled her screen. She tapped to respond, unsure if she could login without connecting to the ship's Wi-Fi system. To her surprise, the app connected immediately.

HASTINGS: Where does Peter hide his blue elephant when he doesn't want to take a nap?

Oops, she'd forgotten to put that on the list of things her sub needed to know. At least the person texting couldn't hear her laugh.

> Dana: Behind the plant in the living room. If you can't find it, ask the AI in the penthouse. She always knows where the elephant is.

The AI Colin Ogilvie designed was scary smart and bordered on creepy sometimes with how much she knew.

> Hastings: Why didn't I think of that?

Acting on a hunch, Dana tapped the reply.

> Dana: ZoElle, is that you?

> Hastings: Yup, the only thing Alan lets me near anymore is the computers. Watching Peter in the apartment qualified as a "safe activity."

> Dana: I won't redefine his definition of safe.

> Hastings 2: How's the trip going?

> Dana: Don't be surprised if there is a viral video of my mother losing it on the plane.

The video phone on the app rang. Dana answered to see ZoElle Hastings, her hair in a messy bun. "I just wanted to wish you bon voyage."

"I'm surprised my app works down here." Dana flipped the camera to show ZoElle the room. "I'm not connected to the ship Wi-Fi and I don't have international data on my phone."

"That isn't the suite you showed me. It looks like a normal—" ZoElle gasped. "—What cruise line are you on?"

Dana held up her key card and panned the room with her phone to show the full effect.

"No wonder I am having flashbacks." ZoElle shuddered. "The kidnappers held us in a room so similar to that one only larger. What happened to the original suite?"

One of Hastings Security's most publicized cases was when ZoElle and Alan posed as newlyweds and rescued an heiress from a deadly situation on a cruise. Who knew it was the same line her sister chose for her bachelorette?

"Motherzilla switched my accommodations. The room is growing on me. Private is good sometimes. Is this the same ship you were on in Panama?"

"I don't know. Definitely the same cruise line. Did you know Colin Ogilvie designed an app for that cruise line about the time Alan and I got married?"

Not surprising that Colin's technology for Hasting Security had been crucial in saving the heiress under their protection. "Is it based on the Hastings app?"

"Probably the same tech. That may be why your app is working on the ship. Colin may have built in a backdoor or something. At least now I know I can contact you if Peter loses anything else."

"And I can contact you if I need to jump ship."

"Is it as bad as you thought it would be?"

"You know my mother. She moved me to this lovely room. Who knows what else she has planned. At least Cheyanne wants me here so…"

ZoElle glanced away from the screen. "They found the elephant. Thanks for letting me bug you on your cruise."

Dana laughed. "I should let you go before I get in trouble with my boss for using the company app when I am on vacation."

"Don't worry about him. Alan is too preoccupied with his impending fatherhood to micromanage the trivial things. Enjoy your cruise!" ZoElle closed the app from her end.

Dana sighed as she lay back on the bed. She reached for her ice pack and the lid fell off spilling cold water and ice on the bed.

It was one of those days, or weeks. Dana cleaned up the best she could. The remaining ice wasn't enough. She needed more. Dana checked the cruise app, there had to be a closer place than by the pool to get ice. An ice machine like a hotel would be nice. If she could wait an hour… no better get it now.

Dana tossed her phone into the fanny pack she wore like a crossbody bag. Her mother had ridiculed the newest fashion, however it was extremely useful with crutches and better than wearing it on her belly or fanny like her mother did. She glanced around the room again for anything she might need. Her key card lay on the bed. She was never that careless. Stress overload? Bad luck? Dana snatched it up and slid it in her pack. She started her second quest for ice.

Four

THE LAST OF THE PASSENGERS filed in. Of the thousands McKay saw today, Dana Knight stood out. Something about her didn't quite fit the typical passenger profile. Maybe it was the way she scanned her surroundings. Something was off.

"Worth." Chief Security Officer Alvaro's voice crackled through his earpiece. "Office."

McKay turned over command to the NECs in charge and hurried to the security office. On the far side of the room, the security crew monitored feeds from nearly three hundred CCTV cameras. He found Alvaro alternating between scanning the screens to checking his tablet, a deep frown etched on his face.

"Sir?"

Alvaro held up the tablet. A notification in a blue box with a familiar logo in the corner illuminated the screen:

HASTINGS Security App Connected: In Use

Hastings Security. The last time he'd heard that name, or seen the blue shield logo, he was a newly minted one-bar security officer on a cruise through the Panama Canal. The private security team had worked with the ship's crew to protect a high-profile passenger. Although the cruise ended well, there had been some tense moments when both a passenger and a Hastings's employee disappeared. McKay checked his phone. The same message appeared.

"Have we had any contact with Hastings? Who are they protecting?" Alvaro asked. He'd been on that ship too. The kidnapping of an oil heiress and the most unassuming security personnel McKay had ever seen resulted in a dramatic rescue and headlines which forced the cruise line to upgrade their security on every ship. "They know to contact us if they're privately hired."

"Contact with who?" asked Martina from her monitoring station, confusion evident in her voice.

The other crew members monitoring the CCTVs stared at him and Alvaro blankly. Only the highest-ranked officers had received the notification.

McKay felt the weight of responsibility settle on his shoulders. At his request the cruise line had shortened his contract by three months. He would be going on leave after this voyage to help his mother. With his brain so full, he didn't need complications.

Alvaro's next words came out in his native Portuguese. Far from fluent in the language, McKay recognized the expletives. "Mac, I hate to ask you, but since you were the only other one on that Panama sailing, will you find the source of this? Confirm they are not providing private security. Call their headquarters in Chicago if necessary. Then find out why our app says this."

"On it."

"Go now. I don't want to pull the anchor until we find the source. The captain will not be happy."

McKay sat at an empty computer terminal and sorted through the passenger list focusing on those who listed home addresses in the greater Chicago area. Forty-three people, including most of the bachelorette party in the Diamond Suite, came up. As did the bride's parents. Dana Knight's reservation was also linked to theirs. McKay read her reservation notes again. That's what had caught his eye when she checked in— originally assigned to the largest suite with the bride, Miss Knight moved three weeks ago to the smallest level of interior rooms on the ship. That was odd. She'd indicated her injury was only a few days old.

After further analysis, three names stood out like buoys in a bay, and one of them belonged to Dana Knight.

Choosing to locate her first had nothing to do with the intelligent gray eyes she'd flashed at him earlier. It was a strategic choice. One, she was the least likely candidate, and Hastings used unlikely bodyguards. Logically, the least likely was the most viable candidate for a Hastings's employee. Two, her crutches would make her easy to find in the ship's security feeds. The CCTV coverage showed her entering her room twenty minutes ago.

McKay headed for the nearest service elevator, his mind racing. If she were here on assignment, he needed to know. If she wasn't... Well, that was a dangerous line of thinking he shouldn't pursue. He hurried along the corridor of deck 8, wishing it had long straight halls like most of the other decks. He turned a corner, only to collide with the woman in question and her crutches.

The impact sent Miss Knight off balance. Her crutches slipped from beneath her. Panic flashed across her face as she teetered. Acting on instinct, McKay reached out quickly, his hands finding purchase on her waist to steady her. Chestnut hair tumbled around her face in waves, and those startling gray eyes peered up at him from mere inches away. A hint of vanilla filled the space between them.

His breath caught. "I am so, so sorry. Are you okay?"

Miss Knight, her chest rising and falling rapidly, met McKay's gaze with a mixture of surprise and the hidden exhaustion many jet-lagged passengers had the first day aboard. "I... I'm fine. Thank you for catching me. I should have been more careful with my crutches."

McKay fought the smile that wanted to answer her as he eased his grip on her waist, making sure she had regained her balance.

The brief contact left his hands tingling. He stepped back, remind-ing himself firmly that she was a passenger or an undercover security officer. Neither option was appropriate for the direction his thoughts wanted to take.

Dana turned sideways in the narrow corridor to allow him to pass. "I'll let you go. You seem to be going somewhere in a hurry."

"Can I help you with anything?"

"No, I was just going to get some ice." Dana scanned the area. "Actually, you're standing on my ice bag. If you could?"

McKay bent for the baby blue bag, noting its medical-grade design. "I can fill it if you would like."

"No, I'm almost to the elevator."

"Why didn't you call room service?"

"For ice? When everyone is hurrying around getting underway..." She looked away as if embarrassed. "And the room service menu said there would be a charge."

"If I take this bag through that 'crew only' door," McKay ges-tured to the door behind her, "I can have it full of ice before you hobble back to your room. And for ice, room service is free." He wasn't exactly sure about the free ice or room service charges. He'd add a note to her profile stating that she shouldn't be charged for ice delivery because of a medical issue.

"How do you know my room—" Dana shook her head. "Never mind. Ship security. You probably know everything about me or would, with a few taps on your phone."

His phone couldn't tell him why her independent nature drew him in. Or what her eyes would look like in candlelight. "How did you know my phone could tell me that?"

She blushed. "Ogilvie Inc. designed your security app. They're the best, so they wouldn't miss a basic detail like that."

Suspicion grew. "How do you know that? Do you work for Hastings Security?"

Dana Knight's eyes narrowed. "Why do you ask?"

A member of housekeeping stepped out of the crew door.

McKay read the name tag and held out the empty ice bag. "Juan, will you please fill this with ice for me?"

"Yes, sir." Juan disappeared back through the door.

"Miss Knight, let me reframe the question. I'm assuming you are employed by Hastings. Did you use your Hastings app on this ship?"

"Yes."

"For what purpose?"

"To answer a work-related question."

Evasive. Not a reason to drag her down to the security office. "Are you here for business or pleasure?"

Dana pointed to her foot. "Do I look like I am here for business?"

The door opened, and Juan handed McKay the ice bag.

"Thank you, Juan. Is Miss Knight's room, 8-1269, one of yours?"

"Yes."

"Will you leave her a bucket of ice at 9 pm?" McKay looked to Dana for confirmation.

"No problem."

"Thank you, Juan. That will be very helpful." Miss Knight graced the steward with a warm smile. How quickly she changed from glaring to kindness. Another red flag.

Juan disappeared back through the crew door.

"Now Miss Knight. I must know, are you on board for business or pleasure?"

"If you must know, I'm here because of my half-sister's wedding, which is definitely not business and, as of yet, very little pleasure."

"Is that why you changed your cabin three weeks ago?"

"I learned this morning that it had been changed. Now are we finished with twenty questions so you can go to wherever you were—" Her eyes narrowed. "You were rushing to find me. Did the Hastings App cause a problem with the ship's security?"

"Not precisely. We received an alert about its use. The chief security officer and I need to be sure you are not working while on board. Last time we ran into—" Unwilling to say more, McKay's voice trailed off.

"This isn't the same ship that was on the Panama cruise was it?"

"No, this one is bigger."

"If it will set your mind at ease, when I used the app earlier and ZoElle Hastings saw my stateroom, she had flashbacks, too. I reassure you, Officer Worth. I am not working. If I were working, your cruise line would have received a call from my employer."

"ZoElle still works for Hastings?" How could he forget such an unusual name?

"Yes." Miss Knight adjusted her grip on her crutches. "Since it made you nervous, I'll promise to not use the app on board again, but I can't guarantee they won't need to contact me."

"Why would they contact you on vacation?"

"I have a very particular principal, and my substitutes have questions that aren't easily answered from the files." She took a hop back. "Well, I'd better get back to my room and ice this ankle."

"Thank you for your time, Miss Knight. Again, I'm sorry I ran into you."

"I can't complain. I got fresh ice and didn't have to go topside again." With a practiced movement, Dana spun on her crutches toward her room.

McKay watched her, unable to look away. Either she was very good at pretending, or she was telling the truth. He would tell Alvaro about their conversation so Alvaro could decide if further action was necessary. Should Miss Knight be allowed to continue the cruise? He wouldn't mind having another spirited exchange with her.

And therein lay the real problem with Miss Knight. He was already thinking about the next time he'd see her, when he should be focusing on security concerns. Five years he'd worked cruise ships without ever being tempted to cross the line with a passenger. What was it about Dana Knight that made him want to risk everything?

The ice bag softened as the cubes melted. Dana adjusted its position, noting her swelling seemed to be going down. Perhaps she should have worn compression socks on the plane, even if they did make her feel like an old lady.

Dana found her thoughts drifting to her encounter with Officer Worth. The way he'd caught her, his hands strong but gentle on her waist... just like that viscount... She shook herself mentally. She was here for Cheyanne's wedding. Besides, cruise ship security officers probably helped dozens of passengers every day. She was just another passenger to him.

Wasn't she? No. She was worse. She reminded him of Panama. Bad memories, that is why he sought her out. And he couldn't fraternize. Seriously she needed to find a new over-the-counter pain med. This one had the side effect of playing cupid.

Someone tapped on the door. One nice thing about the tiny room—Dana didn't have to get up to reach the doorknob. She looked through the peephole relieved to see her sister.

Cheyanne breezed into Dana's cramped stateroom, the air around her shimmering with excitement. She waved a piece of pink paper. "You left the pool before I shared this. I've got everything planned out for the entire trip!"

Dana took the paper and moved closer to the nightstand lamp to read it in the dim room. There had to be a light switch she hadn't located yet.

"Wow," Dana tried to match her sister's energy. "This looks... fun."

"Of course, it is!" Cheyanne sat on the end of the bed, her short pink sundress fluttering around her. "It's my bachelorette cruise. We're going to have the time of our lives."

Dana smiled, genuinely happy to see her sister's excitement. "Agreed."

"You better take care of yourself too, okay? I want you to enjoy this trip just as much as I will, even if you have to miss some things. Like the hike on the cliffs. Chandler and his groomsmen requested that one. He says I can't ignore him the entire time." Cheyanne's smile faltered slightly.

"Walking like a normal person down the aisle in front of you is my number one goal. Don't feel bad if I skip some of the excursions or late-night activities and dancing." Dana held up her phone. "I have a whole TBR selection of books. I won't be bored. And I promise to stay out of Sheila's way so she won't take it out on you."

"Speaking of Mom," Cheyanne tugged at the hem of her dress, "I wanted to apologize for the way she acted on the plane. I can't believe she moved you to this... tiny stateroom, without asking me."

Not a surprise that Chey hadn't known after all. Dana waved off her apology with a wry smile. "No need to apologize, Chey. It's not like it was your fault. I've stayed in worse places."

"I'm glad you had the miles to fly first class. I hope you got some sleep."

A suspicion grew. Their mother's dishonesty reached new depths. At the risk of offending her sister, Dana told the truth. "Actually, I donated most of my miles so Sheila could upgrade you to business. A friend upgraded me."

"What? Chandler paid for my ticket."

Dana pursed her lips, determined to hold in the scream boiling up.

Cheyanne paused her exploration of the room. "Mom's been mean to you over the years. This stinks. I am so sorry."

"I've said it before. It is what it is. You shouldn't have to worry about her issues with me."

"I can't believe Mom moved you to this." Cheyanne waved around the cramped room and leaned over a wall rack to turn on a light.

"Thanks for finding that light switch. This place was giving off a dungeon vibe." Dana tried to lighten the mood. Her mind wandered to Officer Worth's offer to help her get ice. He'd noticed her discomfort before she'd even mentioned it. Stop it, she told herself firmly. Don't go there.

"Chandler's cousin isn't even a bridesmaid. He doesn't even seem to like her. He barely speaks to her. Carlotta is nice and all but she doesn't really belong. I guess that is why she is hanging out with Chandler and the guys, which is what probably annoys Chandler. Erin and Renee are upset about the change too. Especially since your injury is going to exclude you from so much. Amy-Kate and Lindie pointed out it is probably better for you anyway since you don't drink. Which is a stupid thing to get annoyed about. I rarely drink myself, I limit myself to a drink a day. I'm not even sure my mimosa was worth it. But still, we all agree this isn't right."

They were not wrong. "Look at the bright side. No one has to feel bad about having fun while I am sitting on the couch with a bag of ice."

"You don't even have a couch. Oh, but we do have a private hot tub. If it will help your foot, come use it."

"I may take you up on that. Today is my last ice day." Dana pulled out her key card. "I may have to call you though. I bet my card won't access that area."

"Just call or text."

"I need to purchase a shipboard Wi-Fi package. I was counting on the access with the suite. If Mom will pay me the difference, I'll get it today. I know this room was less than my portion of the Diamond Suite.

Cheyanne's eyes widened. "Wait. What? You paid for part of the suite and donated your miles?"

"Yes."

"All the other bridesmaids only paid a thousand for the trip. Daddy covered the rest. This is so wrong."

"I don't care." Or she'd try not to care about the inequity. It was only money. The Ogilvies and their children had taught her money wasn't as valuable as love. Confronting Sheila was likely to result in no refund and even less love. "You know I would do anything to be here."

Chey hugged her. "Don't you dare make me cry. Chandler hates it when I do."

Dana released her sister. "I know this sounds paranoid, but will you check to make sure I have the right dress?"

"Oh no, if Mom…" Cheyanne clapped a hand to her mouth.

"I hung it in the closet."

Cheyanne crossed the few feet to the closet and pulled out the sage dress. "It's perfect."

"Great," Dana said with a sigh of relief. "I have this nightmare of Sheila hijacking our emails."

"Mom is not that tech savvy." Cheyanne pulled out her phone and started tapping. "Speaking of which…I have a couple thousand in my bridal fund left since Chandler's family paid for so much. There. Consider that pay back. We both know Mom won't refund you a penny."

"You don't need to do that."

"Seriously? Yes. I vowed not to be a bridezilla and so far I think I've done pretty good. There was a moment when…" Cheyanne waved her hand in front of her face, pushing the memory aside. "Mom doesn't get to play her games at my wedding even if she is being a, what did you call her, Motherzilla?"

"Pretty much?" asked Dana, trying not to smirk.

"A little. I may have wished for a moment they kicked Mom off the plane. She would have missed the ship. At least she and Daddy are in a different part of the boat. She doesn't have access to my suite either. Daddy said he'd keep her away." Chey giggled. Unlike Dana, she had a good relationship with Mitchell. His best character feature was that he had been too busy to try to take Dana's father's place in her life. When he wasn't working, Cheyanne was his world, even more so than Sheila.

"Alright, I'll take your money," Dana sighed dramatically. "But only because you insist and I am petty too."

Cheyanne's phone pinged. "They are serving dinner in the suite. Do you want to come?"

"I'm sure they only have enough portions for the six of you."

Her sister's arms dropped to her side. "Probably right."

"That is okay. I can go to the buffet and have unlimited desserts."

"As if you would."

"You never know." Dana raised a brow to tease her sister. She looked at her pink paper. "It looks like I get to eat with you tomorrow night. Private banquet at the Ocean's Edge Restaurant."

"Have you seen the photos of it? I love the ice sculptures and everything. Formal just the way Daddy likes it." Cheyanne waved and closed the door behind her.

Dana's stomach rumbled, perhaps she should have two desserts. Using the crutches was bound to burn extra calories. And she could eat away her disappointment in finding a handsome man who was 100% off limits.

Five

McKay leaned back in the security office chair, his eyes glued to the CCTV monitors. Alvaro had assigned him to keep an eye on Miss Knight until they heard from Hastings confirming her story. The captain had left port only ten minutes late, after exclaiming that the sweet woman on crutches couldn't be a threat to his ship. McKay watched her leave her room and head to the buffet. One of the dining rooms closer would have been a better choice, as it didn't require reservations, although it had a long wait time. He shook his head. Not his job to choose her dining options, just observe.

Switching cameras, he followed her progress as she hobbled along to the buffet line, leaning heavily on her crutches while trying to balance a plate in one hand. Where were the workers? The dining staff had crew assigned to help those who might have difficulty navigating the buffet. McKay looked for the radio number for the dining officer and stopped when a crew member stepped up to assist Miss Knight. He frowned that she shouldn't have gotten that far without help.

The security satellite phone rang. Martina answered and handed it to McKay. "Alan Hastings, for you."

McKay took the phone. "Mr. Hastings—"

"Alan, please. My father, Jethro, is Mr. Hastings."

"Thanks for returning my call. I need to confirm that you do have an employee on board, and she is not on duty."

"Why do you think we have an employee on your ship?"

McKay summarized the phone alert and his conversation with Miss Knight.

"Were you on the Panama Canal cruise?"

"Yes, as was the security chief, hence our concern."

"Understandable. I can confirm Miss Knight's conversation with a staff member through our app. She is on PTO. And Hastings has no security work on any of your cruise lines." Alan's voice was firm and friendly. "Our apologies for contacting her through our app and alarming you. I'll have to have my wife look into the app glitch."

"If she is on paid time off, why did you contact her?"

"Um," Alan paused. "Dana's main principles are minors. Not all of them follow predictable patterns. Is that enough for you?"

McKay pictured someone trying to act as security personnel for his niece. "I think I understand. One more question. Miss Knight is on crutches. True or false?"

Alan laughed at this. "Sadly she is, work related injury. One with no principal threat involved. So we can all laugh at the unlikelihood of the accident."

McKay waited a moment for any more disclosures. There were none. "Thank you so much for your time."

"No problem. Sorry we gave you a scare."

"It was the first time I'd seen the name Hastings Security outside of our training videos since Panama."

"You use that scenario for training too?"

McKay smiled. "We learned so much that day."

After ending the call, Martina came to stand behind him. "Should I keep eyes on that woman still?"

"No, need." Shame. McKay didn't mind watching her. She'd been polite to the dining crew members and seemed confident even when dining alone. In his years working for the cruise line, McKay had never come close to even thinking about a passenger in a romantic way. He took one last look at the buffet room camera before standing. "She's not a threat."

McKay texted Alvaro a summary of his discoveries.

Alvaro: Not 100% convinced. PTSD. Monitor from time to time. Her future brother-in-law is a titled and wealthy Brit.

McKay: Will do. Returning to regular duties.

Alvaro sent a thumbs up emoji.

Before leaving the room, McKay scanned the rest of the monitors, looking for signs of trouble. On embarkation day, passengers started drinking earlier than most days. The bar overlooking the main pool was more crowded than normal. A walk through the bars and restaurants might flush out anyone who needed to change to a seat in a food venue.

He hadn't made it halfway through his rounds when he spotted her on the upper deck. Miss Knight leaned against the railing, her crutches propped up beside her, staring out at the horizon where the sinking sun painted the sky in vibrant hues of orange and pink.

He should keep walking. He had actual security concerns to address. Instead, he found himself moving toward her.

"Beautiful sunset, isn't it?" he said, trying to sound casual as he joined her by the railing.

"Oh—hi," She smoothed a hand over her windswept hair. "Yeah, it's beautiful out here."

"Mind if I join you? This is my last cruise for a while. Wanted to get in more sunsets before I head home."

Miss Knight's eyes flicked away from the view, and she looked him over with a hint of amusement. "You mean you're not here to keep tabs on me?"

The knowing look in her eyes told him she'd been aware of the surveillance. Of course she had. She was a security professional herself. Something about that made her even more intriguing. Most passengers either never noticed they were being watched or became paranoid when they did. He was entering turbulent waters. He needed to maintain professional distance. Instead, he found himself drawn into conversation with her, wanting to know more about the woman who could spot surveillance and make jokes about it. Would a life preserver save him?

"No. I spoke with Alan Hastings. I'm not concerned about you causing trouble."

"To be fair, it wasn't Alan or ZoElle or anyone from Hastings Security that caused trouble on a cruise. They only stopped it."

"Touché." McKay leaned on the railing next to her. "I'm not worried about you starting any trouble."

"You realize that if I saw an incident, I'd be compelled to stop it, or at least report it."

"The job never leaves, does it?"

"Does it leave you?" She answered his question with one of her own. Telling him more than a straight answer would. She didn't trust him yet. "Where is home?"

"Indiana. As land locked as one can be."

"Nope, still have the Great Lakes. I'd say Wyoming wins."

"Or Colorado."

"South Dakota."

He couldn't help smiling. "Well, now that we both know our geography…"

Miss Knight reached for crutches. One fell to the deck. McKay bent for it at the same time she did, knocking her off her foot. She landed with a thud.

"Sorry." Instinctively, he knelt by her side.

"I'm fine. Only thing wounded is my pride. I'll be so happy to be off these things."

McKay pulled over a deck chair and helped her up.

"Still believe I am in some disguise?" Miss Knight checked her splinted foot. "Right now, you're probably wondering why Alan Hastings lets me out in the field."

"He was laughing about your injury on the phone."

"I was playing soccer with my principals. A gopher hole jumped in my way."

"And here I thought security details usually stood around all day."

"Some do." She turned her head to the sunset. "What's waiting for you back home?"

"Family, mostly. My mom and sister need some help." He debated about telling her more. If the situation were different, he might say she was easy to talk to. "I'm taking several months leave."

"Serious problems?"

"Enough." Time to change the subject. "I don't see you hanging out with your family."

"You've been watching." Not a question. She looked up at him, her eyes narrowing.

"Just until we had confirmation from Hastings Security. Why did you choose the buffet?"

"Because I wasn't thinking logistics. Hopefully, I am off these in a few days."

"Next nosey question. You are part of the big bridal party. Why aren't you with them?"

"Tonight? They are in the casino. I'd rather go put my foot up and read. My sister urged me to go. She's a good kid."

"But?"

"My mother is the Motherzilla-of-the-bride." The nickname wasn't a bad replacement for Momster.

"Motherzilla? Is that like Godzilla?"

"Something like that. In case you haven't guessed, I am not the favorite child."

"Why is that?"

"I was four when Dad came home from deployment. I mentioned I loved him more than my other 'daddy'... the divorce was completed before he served ten years, which makes a big difference in the alimony. When I was ten, I fought for a change of custody so I could go live with him. I spent as little time as possible after that with my mother and Mitchell. Cheyanne and I have only gotten to know each other these last four years."

McKay's respect for her grew. It couldn't have been easy standing up to family at such a young age. "That is an interesting dynamic."

"My Dad is great. He retired from the military and took a job as a policeman in the town where my Mother lives just to be near me. He never missed a single school event, or anything."

"And your Mother did?"

She shrugged a shoulder and looked out to sea again.

"Sorry, I didn't mean to—" McKay stepped back both emotionally and physically. He should go. He was on duty and any justification that this conversation was a soft interrogation was flimsy at least.

Miss Knight shrugged. "Most lives are complicated, aren't they? Sorry, I shouldn't have told you all of that."

"Sometimes talking to a stranger is better than therapy."

For a moment, they sat in silence, each lost in their own thoughts as they watched the sun disappear below the horizon.

McKay found himself wanting to tell her about his mother's illness, about why he was really leaving the ship. Something about Dana Knight made him want to open up, and that was exactly why he needed to maintain his distance.

"Officer Worth," she began hesitantly. "I just wanted to say thank you. For your kindness today. You could have tossed me overboard."

McKay chuckled. "We usually ask people to walk the plank, but when I saw those crutches, well I didn't have the heart to."

As darkness settled around them, the ship's lights twinkled like stars against the inky sky.

"It's so peaceful out here." She rubbed her arms, calming a shiver. "Hard to believe we're on a giant ship with thousands of people when it feels this serene."

McKay nodded, also taking in the magnificent scene. "It's one of my favorite parts of working on a cruise. No matter how hectic the day is, I know I can come out here and just watch the sunset and relax."

The way the fading light illuminated Miss Knight's face, even exhausted from a long day and hobbling around on crutches, radiated something special. A beauty he couldn't let get under his skin. "Back home, I'm lucky to get a chance to catch a sunset over the cornfields. This definitely beats Indiana."

Miss Knight laughed, her nose wrinkling up in amusement. "Chicago sunsets have their appeal too, when you can actually see the sky through all the buildings. But this is pretty hard to beat."

They stood for a minute longer, the silence comfortable between them.

"I should go. My ice should be in my room by now and I need to get my foot back up."

"May I walk you back? I wouldn't want you to fall again."

She stood balanced on the crutches he handed her. "Oddly enough, the only times I've fallen or run into someone, you've been around."

"Is that a no?"

She laughed, a clear, crisp sound. "I can't really stop you, can I? But seeing that the boat is rocking more than when I came up. I can't say I wouldn't mind a spotter. If I injure myself again, my mother will start breathing fire."

"We can't have that. I don't know if you've noticed, but fire and cruises don't mix well."

When they arrived at her room, Miss Knight paused in the hallway outside her cabin door. "Thanks for tonight. It was really nice talking to you."

"My pleasure." McKay smiled. "Perhaps I'll run into you again."

"Please, not literally."

"No. Not that. If you need more ice or assistance, just ring your cabin steward."

"I will."

They stood as if frozen, unable to avoid the awkward end. Then McKay cleared his throat. "Well, goodnight, Miss Knight. Sleep well."

He walked on down the passageway, listening for the click of her door. He'd come too close to the line he'd set for himself with passenger relations tonight. He shouldn't be interested in her. Alvaro needed to be content that she wasn't here for anything other than the wedding, so he wouldn't have another excuse to talk with her. Perhaps he could look her up when they were home. It was only a three-hour drive to Chicago, if traffic was good.

Dana shut her cabin door and leaned against it, her heart racing in a way that had nothing to do with navigating on crutches. She'd just flirted with a crew member. Worse, she'd enjoyed it. What was she thinking?

She wasn't thinking; that was the problem. He'd remained mostly professional. Minus the whole walking her back to the room thing. Which she could chalk up to a liability thing especially after toppling over on deck. Her life couldn't handle much more embarrassment. Falling all over a handsome man. At least her training kicked in and she'd changed her trajectory to the deck. The memory of his hands on her hips earlier today was enough. She didn't need to end up in his arms again.

She placed her crutches on the floor under the bed. His excuse to walk her back was mostly legitimate. She should have waved him off when they reached her hall and avoided that awkward first date door moment. First date? She'd never told a first date so much about her life.

Jet lag. It had to be jet lag. Maybe the jokes about the Love boat. Flirting with—forget flirting—trusting. She'd gone straight to trusting him. It took her days, if not weeks, to trust her very well vetted coworkers. And she couldn't remember telling any of them that much about her family. She'd spent hundreds of hours on duty with Chris, and he didn't know half as much about her.

The bucket of ice sat in the bathroom sink. A good place in rough seas, she supposed. There was enough for 2 ice packs.

After changing and brushing her teeth, she made her way to the bed and settled in with her ice pack. She searched her reading app for *Persuasion*. After watching it the other night, she wanted to review the finer points. The words on her phone faded as she replayed her conversation with Officer Worth. The way he half smiled when she teased him about following her.

Her phone buzzed, breaking her out of her dangerous thoughts.

Brit: How's the cruise so far? Meet any handsome officers?

Dana groaned. Of course Brit would ask that. She typed back:

Dana: Getting ready to go to bed. Sheila caused drama on the plane. Did Simone tell you?

Brit: That's not an answer to my second question.

Writing her answer, Dana remembered she hadn't paid for ship Wi-Fi. She checked to make sure the Hastings app was off. She didn't need Officer Worth banging on the door when she was in her comfy t-shirt featuring a hippo eating chocolate, and boy shorts.

Dana: We discussed that impossibility.

Brit: Rumor has it, the cruise ship called Hastings.

How did she know that? Of course Mr. Gossip himself. One of these days…

> Dana: Doesn't Javier have something better to do than gossip?

> Brit: I think you are being too evasive.

> Dana: Yes, I met and was questioned by an officer. They were worried I was a security risk.

> Brit: My imaginary version is better.

It was tempting to ask what her friend imagined just so she could compare.

> Dana: I'm here for Chey's wedding. That's all.

> Brit: Was he cute?

> Dana: Who?

> Brit: The officer who interrogated you?

Not cute. Handsome.

> Dana: Doesn't matter, he is an employee.

> Brit: Hmmmmm.

> Dana: Good night. It is past bedtime here.

> Brit: Night. Sweet dreams… of ship's officers.

Dana dropped her phone on the bed. She didn't need her friends encouraging this. Whatever it was. She was here for Cheyanne's wedding. She needed to focus on being a good sister and bridesmaid, not mooning over a security officer like some romance novel heroine.

Giving up on reading, Dana turned off the app and dreamed the exact dreams Brit wished upon her.

Six

THE SMALL LOBBY OUTSIDE THE ship's exclusive upscale restaurant screamed ambiance. Dana joined her sister and the other bridesmaids in the corner of the waiting area. Like her, they'd all worn their little black dresses for dinner. The elevator opened and Chandler stepped off with the groomsmen. The other elevator opened, and the parents of the bride exited chatting. Cheyanne's father approached the podium, and the group lined up behind him.

The hostess looked at her screen, then back at the group. "Sir, your reservation is for fourteen. There are fifteen here."

Sheila looked behind her and counted. She stopped when her eyes met Dana's. "I did not invite you to this event."

Cheyanne's mouth dropped. "What do you mean? Of course, Dana is invited. She is my sister and a bridesmaid."

"But she isn't in the room with you and we used your room dining credit for part of this meal."

"She was in the room until you kicked her out." Cheyanne's voice rose.

Dana hopped a step forward and put her hand on her sister's arm. "It's okay. Obviously, a mistake was made. I'll go eat elsewhere."

"You shouldn't have to. You are all dressed up after our spa day." Cheyanne turned to the hostess. "Can you add an extra chair?"

"No, she can't." Sheila cut off the hostess's response. "It would be an odd number."

Chandler's cousin Carlotta waved her hand. "I'm not really in the bridal party…"

"Nonsense, you're Chandler's family. You must stay." Sheila narrowed her eyes at Dana as if daring her to point out that she was family, too.

Filet mignon, or whatever else was on the menu, wasn't worth the fight and the bad feelings that would continue throughout the meal. "I really should go ice my ankle soon. I'll just grab a quick bite at the buffet. Go, enjoy."

Cheyanne pursed her lips and leaned closer to Dana's ear. "You shouldn't give in to her on this."

"Sometimes it is better to retreat. It is only a dinner." Dana watched Cheyanne and the rest of the group enter the restaurant in the reflection of the mirrored wall. She closed her eyes for a moment, willing the pain that had been her constant companion since she was five-years old to go away. She wasn't that hungry anyway.

"Miss Knight?" An officer she'd noticed entering the restaurant earlier approached. "I'm Officer Alvaro, head of Security. I would like to extend my apologies for having Officer Worth investigate you."

Dana managed a small smile. "No problem. Actually, it turned out quite helpful to discover I could order ice whenever I needed it."

"I noticed a bit of commotion just now from my seat at the captain's table, that left you without dinner." Alvaro's voice had a mild soothing accent to it. "The captain's table is one guest short due to sea sickness. He asked me to issue an invitation for you to join us. Officer Worth, is also with us, so you will know another face."

"After the trouble I've given you, I should say no."

"I would consider it a crime for a beautiful woman dressed for a celebration to eat alone," Chief Security Officer Alvaro coaxed.

Dana adjusted her crutches. "I wouldn't want to commit a crime onboard. I already have security suspicious."

Alvaro smiled broadly. "I would offer my arm but," his words trailed off as he winked and tipped his head towards her crutches.

Dana followed him as he wound through the dining room, the faint strains of a live string quartet grew. Her crutches sank into the soft carpet as they wound their way around the tables to the largest table with a view of the sea. The captain and other male officers stood as she neared. Officer Worth came to the end of the dais and offered her a hand up and into the chair he'd pulled out. A bus boy took her crutches and laid them behind the platform, well out of the way.

Even Brit's imagination couldn't have put Dana dining at the captain's table next to a handsome and single officer.

The captain retook his seat as did the others. "Miss Knight. Thank you for joining us on short notice. I'm afraid we've already made introductions and had appetizers in my cabin. If you could introduce yourself, we'll go around again briefly."

Dana hoped none of the stress from moments before showed on her face. Her brain was torn between acknowledging the honor of eating at the captain's table and the mortification of being saved. She gave an introduction so generic it could have been printed on an off-brand cereal box. She struggled to remember the names as others gave hurried introductions. The couples closest to here were, the Jacksons from Toledo who were celebrating their sixtieth wedding anniversary, and the Murres, from Spain, who were celebrating their honeymoon.

A waiter handed her a menu.

Officer Worth leaned over. "The rest of us have chosen our courses. If you'll point out your choices to the waitstaff, they'll get your order prepared as well."

Wishing she could ponder the items, Dana picked quickly, assuming everyone would have to wait on her before being served their first course. Her hand shook as she pointed out the items.

"Relax, other than this table, there are only three people paying attention to the fact you entered the room. And your sister looks quite pleased," said Officer Worth in a low voice.

The other two had to be Sheila and Mitchell. Dana resisted the urge to look at their table.

Officer Worth asked both couples how they met. The Jacksons met at an Elvis concert. Mr. Jackson even did a reasonable impersonation of the famous singer. "Thank you, thank you very much." The Murres stopped staring into each other's eyes long enough to say they met on a dating app.

The first course was served, and Dana's shoulders relaxed as the meal continued. The captain answered questions about the roughest seas he'd encountered and the friendly dolphin who seemed to always greet him at a port in Australia.

Mrs. Jackson leaned close. "So how did you meet the handsome security officer, shoplifting?"

"Nothing like that. There was a cell phone glitch when we were still in port that set off their security protocols. A one-in-a-million random event."

"This cruise is not lucky for you?" asked the new bride in beautifully accented English. Dana couldn't understand the woman's grammar and if Mrs. Murre was saying she was lucky or unlucky.

"I can't say unlucky. I may be on crutches, but I get to eat at the captain's table." Dana smiled.

"I'd say it is very lucky, since you also get to sit next to the most handsome man at the table." Mrs. Jackson winked. "Next to my David, of course."

Dana took a bite of food to avoid responding. This was not some 1980s television show. Officer Worth was not vacation romance material. Well, he was, but unlike the sitcom, he was off limits. And even if there was a small likelihood they could meet up after the cruise; well it was best to not think or act on any attraction she may or may not be feeling. "Yes. I have all the luck of the Irish with me on this cruise."

Next to her, Officer Worth laughed. "I believe the cruise director made that the theme of the cruise."

Mr. Murre nodded in the direction of Cheyanne's table. "But your own group refused to let you in with their party. Not very lucky."

Before Dana could think of a response, the captain answered from the end of the table. "Which makes ours the luckier table. And reminds me, I have reserved some VIP tickets for tonight's show for the passengers in this group."

The octogenarian sitting next to him clapped her hands and others followed. Dana had no idea what the show was, but she clapped too. The conversation turned to the show and the singer's reputation.

Dana savored the Beef Wellington as she listened to the others talk.

"Enjoying dinner?" asked Officer Worth.

"It is divine. I can't help but be happy that some poor person had sea sickness."

"It happens. Have you had any trouble?"

Dana raised her hand to her neck, not quite touching the patch behind her ear. "Alan Hastings warned me about this and suggested I get the anti-nausea patches. I may be over medicating myself as I put one on before coming onboard. But, I decided I couldn't take the risk."

"I knew you were a wise woman."

"Really? I thought I was a security risk."

"A wise one." His smile was like a warm hug. Seriously, did he flirt with every passenger like this? Dance right up to the no consorting rule and leave a trail of broken hearts?

Dana turned back to her plate. Just her luck. The guy was off limits. If he had been a regular passenger, she probably wouldn't find him attractive. She repeated the lie to herself, hoping to believe it. Someone cleared her plate and replaced it with dessert. It looked too pretty to sink her fork into.

Next to her, Mrs. Jackson gasped. "Oh, I love this dessert so much. Too bad they only serve it in this restaurant."

Mr. Jackson chuckled. "You wouldn't like it half as much if it were on the buffet for everyone to get. Part of what makes it special is it is a rare commodity."

"You can take the professor of economics out of the university, but you can't take the economics out of the professor." Mrs. Jackson covered her husband's hand with her own.

Dana had the distinct impression this was not the first time the older woman had said this. Everyone else picked up their forks and most of them were enjoying the decadent treat.

"Is something wrong?" Officer Worth nodded to her dessert.

"It is almost too pretty to ruin by eating."

"You won't think that after your first bite," said Mrs. Murre. She closed her eyes as if she'd been transported to another level of consciousness.

Dana cut out a piece with her fork and added one of the fresh raspberries. The others were right. Words couldn't describe the perfection of the chocolate and berry dessert.

"Told you it was good," said Mrs. Jackson.

"Good is not an adequate word." Dana savored a second bite. Across the room, Chey waved a subtle gesture as she and the others prepared to leave. Sheila glared. Dana closed her eyes. Her mother would not ruin this moment for her. Chocolate and a handsome man. Both would be gone soon, but for now, they were hers.

The passengers finished up their meals, and each was given a small blue folder with a ticket to the evening's performance, a commemorative menu, and a photo with the captain, Dana's photo spot was empty.

"Miss Knight. Do you mind if we take the photo here?" asked the captain.

"Of course not."

Officer Worth helped Dana stand and helped her with her crutches so she could move to the head of the table. "Do you want me to hold your crutches, or do you want them to be part of the memory?"

"I think they should be part of it."

The captain stood by her side as the ship's photographer took the photo. "I think you should also have one with our security team."

Officer Alvaro took a place on the other side of the captain, and Officer Worth stood beside her for the next photo.

"Thank you for joining us tonight." The captain shook Dana's hand.

Standing near where the captain had sat all evening Dana realized that the arrangement of the mirrors allowed the captain to see out into the small lobby by the hostess stand. She nodded to the mirrors. "Thank you for allowing me to join your group."

"I should have known you'd find my secret. We are the fortunate ones this evening." The captain smiled. "Now, if you will excuse me, I must get back to the bridge."

Officer Alvaro nodded to her. "I also must go. Officer Worth will escort you to the theater or wherever you planned on going. We entered rougher waters during the meal, and I remember having to use crutches in my youth."

"Thank you."

Officer Worth touched her elbow to spot her as she descended the dais. "It may be easier to go around the far wall since the aisle is wider there."

Dana moved her crutches, breaking the contact of his fingers with her elbow. The spot tingled all the way to the elevator.

What was Alvaro thinking? Escort a passenger? They rarely did that. Of course, he hadn't told Alvaro that Dana offered a threat in a different direction than they originally thought. McKay cleared his throat. "To the theater?"

"Is the show any good?" Miss Knight's black dress swirled above her knees.

He looked away while adding her legs to the list of things he shouldn't notice. "Yes."

The elevator arrived empty. A blessing or curse, given how conscious he was of their proximity.

"Why security?" he asked as the doors closed.

"My father is a police officer. I intended to follow him, but life took a turn." She adjusted her grip on the crutches. "I could ask you the same thing."

"I love the sea. After the Navy, security was a natural progression. Definitely not a boring desk job."

"I'm sure you have some stories."

"A few. Though probably nothing compared to whatever you're not telling me about your work."

"Officer Worth…"

"McKay, most people call me McKay. Or Mac."

Her eyes softened. "McKay. Thank you for the escort."

The elevator reached the deck where the theater was located. McKay walked her to the door of the theater closest to the VIP seating. "Enjoy the show, Miss Knight."

"Dana," she offered with a small smile. "Since we're exchanging names."

"Good evening, Dana."

McKay walked around the deck before slipping into an employee corridor and back to the security office.

Alvaro was exiting as he arrived. "I'm up to the casino to deal with a problem. Did you get Miss Knight to the theater?"

"Yes. Why did you have me escort her? And don't tell me about crutches. If we had to escort every person with a cane on board, we would never do another thing."

His friend smiled. "Honestly? I was worried her family might be waiting to pounce on her and I don't think she deserves it."

"Oh, I thought—" McKay shook his head. There was no reason to disclose his feelings. "Never mind."

Alvaro nodded and continued on his way. McKay shook his head again. What had he been thinking? There was no way the chief security officer would have tried to set him up with a passenger and break policies they were both paid to enforce.

McKay took the chair in the back of the room that oversaw all the other security personnel watching the monitors.

From his control chair, he checked the cameras the security crew had flagged for monitoring. A table in the casino, a table in the top side bar, a man and a woman in a secluded area of the ship. Only shadows moved on screen as there was a two-yard-long blind spot there. The largest one in the passenger areas. Few people knew where the blind spots were in the CCTV coverage, so any time people lingered in one, it was concerning.

McKay sent a message to the closest security member to take a walkthrough of the corridor in question. A moment later, a couple emerged from the shadows. McKay zoomed in on them. Wasn't that Miss Knight's future brother-in-law? The red head was not the bride-to-be.

The security crew messaged back that the area was clear and the couple had moved on. No evidence of assault. Which had been the original concern. Nothing illegal, not his problem.

Three hours later, alone in his cabin, the incident with the fiancé still bothered him. It wasn't uncommon to see evidence of unfaithfulness onboard. Maybe it was the fact that the groom knew or guessed a spot where the CCTV coverage had a small break, or maybe it was his relationship with Dana.

The nightly call with Gracie and Jen interrupted his thoughts. Gracie showed him her countdown calendar for going to Robyn's Place. She'd added a big red heart for next Wednesday.

"Do you know what this is?" Gracie pointed to the heart.

"No."

"It's the day you come home!"

On her calendar, it seemed so close. "Actually, that is the day the cruise ends. I have to go sign some papers and things. I'll likely be home on Friday."

"Do you know your flight yet?" asked Jen.

"I'm sure I have an email about it." The cruise line would book his flight, so he had thought little of it.

Jen rolled her eyes. "I don't get how you can be so responsible most of the time and other times not seem to care."

"I do care. My flight isn't one of those things I need to worry about today. Someone else is making the reservations. I'm having a harder time packing up all my stuff. I'm going to have an extra suitcase as it is."

"Mom was talking about one of those rings you can get in Ireland again today. I assume you'll have room for one?"

"Claddagh ring, right?"

Jen nodded.

"What are you bringing me, Uncle Mac?"

Jen turned to her daughter and frowned. "Gracie, that is rude. We don't expect gifts from Mac just because he is coming home."

"But he always brings me something."

Mac laughed. "I may not bring you anything this time."

"Please? Uncle Mac. I won't ask." Gracie cringed with an almost innocent smile.

"If I have room in my suitcase. Jen, do you have any requests?"

"The usual." His sister was easy. She always wanted the local chocolate.

"Not a problem. I'll bring you Irish and British Cadbury. I heard they are slightly different."

"I can't wait to test that."

Gracie exaggerated a yawn. "It's my bedtime. When I wake up, I can mark off another day."

"Good night." McKay blew a kiss to his niece.

Jen waited until a door closed in the background to speak. "If I'd known how this calendar would have changed our bedtime drama, I would have tried one earlier. She loves marking off the days."

"How is Mom?"

"As far as I can tell, she is hopeful. They scheduled her surgery for a week from Tuesday to give you a few extra days to get back."

"Mom assumes every flight will be canceled, doesn't she?"

"It happens often enough."

The last three times he'd taken leave, something had gone wrong with his flight. "Fair."

Jen bit her lip.

"What is it?"

"Mom is lining dates up for you."

"How bad this time?"

"So far, a nurse and a niece of one of her friends. She hasn't started in on my coworkers yet."

McKay took a deep breath. "I should have expected as much. Don't worry, I'll let her have some fun before I put an end to it. Besides, it might be nice to talk to a woman without worrying about crossing invisible lines."

"Work rules?"

"Yup." McKay opened his mouth to say something about Dana and stopped at the last second.

Jen's eyes narrowed. "Who is she? Passenger or crew?"

Technically, he could date crew if they were not subordinates. Which in the end only left one or two female crew members and the drama wouldn't be worth it. "I didn't say there was someone."

"But there is. I can tell. I haven't seen that smile for a very long time."

"She is pretty, intelligent, and she's nice. Nothing more, no lines crossed. Not going to cross them."

"Nothing saying you can't call her when you are back here. You could get her number."

"Maybe. But we still have seven days onboard and I shouldn't even think of it."

A grin grew on Jen's face. "Wow. I never thought I'd see the day."

"There is nothing to see. Nothing happening." He made a show of looking at his watch. "I should call Mom now."

Jen laughed and waved goodbye.

McKay made it through his call with his mother, avoiding the topic of women and dating. Probably because his mother didn't dare bring up that she was already planning dates for him, and she was more worried that he wouldn't arrive before her surgery.

When the call was over, McKay laid back on his bed and closed his eyes. An image of Dana filled his mind. There was a dignity about how she carried herself even on crutches, even with her family basically shunning her. It was a quality he'd not thought of before in a woman. Perhaps that is what made her stand out. The last night of the cruise, he would ask for her number. Until then, he would avoid her. It was best for both of them.

Seven

THE LINE TO THE TINDER boats wound down the hallway. For the first time since boarding, Dana was truly annoyed with her mother for switching her out of the premium suite. Her sister and the other bridesmaids had received VIP treatment and disembarked forever ago without waiting in the line. A crew member came down the line checking excursion tickets. Dana held out hers.

The young man looked at the crutches. "Come with me, please."

He led Dana to a much shorter line filled with people on scooters. "Since you are using crutches, you can use this line. Can you navigate the stairs without help?"

"Yes." A stab of guilt ran through Dana; this line was for those with limited mobility. Her crutches qualified? A minute later, she was at the front of the line, where a crew member took her crutches. The stairs down to the tinder boat moved with the waves. Dana gripped the rails tightly, glad that she could bear some weight on her injured ankle as she hopped down the short flight. At home, she would have ditched the crutches by now. However, she did not know how much she would need to walk today and erred on the side of caution.

The cramped tinder boat bobbed in the water. Passengers squeezed together like the proverbial sardines on hard molded benches. Dana hoped those facing her wouldn't discover they were seasick now.

No one did.

At the port, a bus making the drive to Waterford waited. A large van, that had begun to pull out, stopped suddenly in front of the bus. The door flew open and her sister jumped out.

"Dana!" Cheyanne waved her arms. "Where were you? Come on!"

Dana hurried over at Olympic speed, if crutch running was a sport.

Cheyanne gave her a quick side hug as they found their seat on the bus. "I'm so glad you made it. Next time come up to the suite and you can leave with us. I asked about it this morning."

From the seat behind them, their mother scoffed as the van began moving again and turned on to the main road. The conversation quickly turned to what type of crystal Cheyanne wanted. As they drove through the picturesque countryside of Ireland, Dana found herself lost in thought, wondering about the people who lived here for centuries.

Cheyanne's excited squeal interrupted Dana's daydreams. "Look! There it is!" Cheyanne pointed at a sign that read "Waterford Crystal Visitors Centre."

The van pulled into a parking spot on the street and they all piled out. The visitors centre was bustling with people. A young woman who was checking group's tour times approached them.

"Welcome to the Visitors Centre," she said. "Feel free to look around and let us know if you have any questions before your tour."

The group wandered around the gift shop, admiring the sparkling crystal pieces on display.

As Dana approached the crystal saxophone to get a better look at the masterpiece, Sheila called out, "Careful on your crutches. I'm not paying for anything you break."

Not wanting to cause a scene, Dana gave her mother a tight-lipped smile and turned back to admire the glass cutter's work.

Their tour was called, and their guide introduced himself as he led them into the factory. As a former artisan, his presentation was full of insight as he showed them the various craftsmen working on their latest creations. Dana marveled at the precision and skill it took to turn a raw piece of crystal into something so beautiful. Skilled woodcarvers created moulds for glassblowers to shape the red-hot glass. Others hand-marked the glass for the cutters to carve the intricate patterns into the crystal. Sculptors made some unique pieces by shaping the glass. Having barely mastered making snakes and bowls from children's clay, the amount of skill required to sculpt a block of glass into a gramophone or other unique item awed Dana.

The tour ended back in the shopping gallery. Dana wanted to purchase some small item to remember the skill of those who worked years to make something out of glass. Cheyanne and her bridesmaids gathered to choose a set of champagne glasses. Dana wandered in search of something that better fit her style. Nothing too ornate, but a piece that would show off the craft and skills she'd witnessed. And most of all, something that fit her budget. After considering various Christmas ornaments, picture frames and clocks, she settled on a small crystal bowl that had heart-shaped sides.

The piece was beyond what she'd budgeted, but with the money Chey had given her she could splurge a little. Dana found an employee to assist her since balancing on her crutches and picking up a piece of crystal were not activities she was going to try at the same time.

At a nearby register, Sheila and Mitchell argued over how much to spend on Cheyanne's gift. The bridesmaids rushed out of the shop as if they heard a fire alarm, leaving the maid of honor to help Chey. Dana followed behind.

"Hey Dana, want to go with us to the Viking tower?" Lindie, who had been Cheyanne's roommate, pointed to the end of the street. "We have an hour before the van comes back."

Dana gauged the distance to be less than the length of the cruise ship. "Sure, let's go."

On the way down, they ran into Chandler and his minions. They dressed more alike than the women, each man duplicating Chandler's style.

"Where is Cheyanne?" asked Chandler.

Lindie nodded to the Waterford building. "I wouldn't go there. Her mother is trying to get her to buy this set of crystal she doesn't want."

"She doesn't need any. My mum has three sets. I told your mum this three times." He hurried up the hill.

"No offense, Dana, but your mom is kind of a mess." Amy-Kate grimaced. "I thought Cheyanne exaggerated all these years, about how controlling she could be, but not so much."

Dana had only met Amy-Kate a handful of times. Her ginger hair made her easy to remember. "Not offended."

"She's been pretty awful to you this trip. I was secretly cheering for you when you ended up at the captain's table. And sitting next to that hot guy. I am a sucker for a man in uniform." Lindie hummed her appreciation. "Are you going to try to see him again?"

"Officer Worth works security. I'm sure we will all see him from time to time, especially when we board the ship." Dana watched her feet to not put her crutches in one of the many cracks between the cobblestones.

Lindie threw up her hands. "That isn't what I meant and you know it."

"He's got to be thirty, just the right age for you." Erin's comment could have been taken as an insult, but Dana ignored it. Oh to be twenty again.

"In case you missed it in all your information from the cruise, crew members are not to be involved with passengers." Amy-Kate's voice held a note of superiority which poked Dana the wrong way.

"I'm not sure it would stop me." Erin tossed her obviously dyed red hair over her shoulder. "I'm with Lindie, I love me a man in uniform."

"It does me." Dana hoped to end the speculation. "If I liked Officer Worth, I wouldn't want to jeopardize his job."

"If?" said Lindie with a grin. "Only an 'if?'"

They reached the bottom of the hill where an ancient tower built by the Vikings stood. Dana changed the subject. "That door seems awfully short. I always thought the Vikings were tall."

Erin pointed to a model of a ship on the far side of the tower. "I thought their ships were bigger, too."

"There has got to be some information around here to read." Dana's search for a sign took her a few steps from the other women. As she read, they were joined by Cheyanne and Renee. The poor maid of honor looked exasperated. Dana wished she could help, but her interference in the shop would have made things worse. It seemed Chandler charging into the shop had ended the standoff. After a few minutes of looking around the Viking tower, the group returned to the visitors centre to await their ride. When the van returned they all slowly piled in.

To Dana's relief, no one mentioned Officer Worth again. The last thing she needed was Lindie and her friends deciding to make sure she saw more of him.

Excited passengers returned from their first at shore day. Most were too excited to complain about long lines or the need to return early. As usual, a few passengers ignored the regulations on food and other prohibited items. McKay stood between the check in scanner and the X-ray machine, ready to intervene if necessary. Over the years, he'd learned that most of those who tried to bring fruits, meat, or dairy products on board were fully aware they shouldn't and a stern glare with his arms crossed would keep them from arguing with the security staff. The few passengers that purchased souvenirs in the form of Irish Whisky or other drinks registered their purchases to be held until the end of the cruise.

A blue-haired lady and her friend stopped in front of him. She held up a candy bar. "Sir, we purchased chocolate. Do you need to confiscate it?"

"No, ma'am. Chocolate is not prohibited. You may bring as much as you wish."

She turned to her friend. "I told you chocolate isn't food."

"Chocolate is food. And no one needs as much as you purchased."

The pair continued to the x-ray station.

McKay hid his smile as he glanced at the monitor and saw what looked to be five or more pounds of chocolate in blue-hair's purse.

The next tinder boat arrived, and a crew member ran a pair of crutches up to the top of the stairs. Unless someone injured themselves at port, there was only one passenger on the ship who could be coming his way soon. He paid more attention to the boarding passengers than he did the ones having their belongings scanned. The fiancé, the bride-to-be, the mother, and several other bridesmaids came up the ladder. Was that the same redhead from last night? Or was it that one? He'd already counted a half dozen ginger haired possibilities.

Dana was the last one up the stairs. Of course, she would have voluntarily come last.

"Miss Knight, how was your ashore day?"

"Very nice, thank you."

Two bridesmaids giggled, and Dana blushed.

Not good.

McKay knew he hadn't crossed any lines. But perhaps he had stepped too close. No more special treatment for Dana. He turned his attention to the crew members at the alcohol check-in table. He had a job to do. If he had three months left on his contract or if Dana lived on the other side of the country, like in Idaho, it would be easier to ignore her. Knowing that he could see her again was likely what fueled the attraction. He needed to ignore it.

Still, McKay found his attention drifting to the door Dana had disappeared through. The next passengers approached with shopping bags full of souvenirs, but he barely registered their presence. What was it about Dana Knight that made maintaining professional distance so difficult? In five years of working cruise ships, he'd never been tempted to cross that line. Now he wanted to run across the finish line, arms raised up high like a marathon winner.

"Sir?" A passenger's voice snapped him back to attention. "Do I need to register this bottle?"

McKay forced himself to focus on his duties. He couldn't afford to be distracted, especially not by a passenger.

Eight

Without crutches, the cobblestone streets and walk-ways of Galway were fairly simple to navigate. Dana stopped at the first shop she came to. Alone for the day, she intended to find an Irish wool sweater for herself and one for her father, if she could. She was in no rush. Cheyanne, Chandler, and the rest of the party had hurried to see the Claddagh rings before taking an all-day tour of the Cliffs of Moher, which included a two-mile hike. While she was more than glad to ditch the crutches, a hike was more than she should take on, since the goal was to stand at her sister's wedding in heels.

She wandered in and out of the shops in the tourist trap district. One shop boasted the softest sweaters in town. Dana browsed each shelf until she'd seen every sweater. A traditional Aran sweater caught her eye. Knowing she would come back the same way to return to the dock, Dana left without making a purchase. What were the chances that the first store would have the perfect sweater? Better off checking the other stores before settling on this one.

Two streets later, a jewelry shop tempted her inside with its promise of sitting for a twenty-minute presentation on Claddagh rings. It was time for a rest.

After watching a video presentation on the history of the Claddagh ring and its symbols of the heart, hands, and crown. She politely looked at the less expensive rings in the shop before exiting. Since the ring's history was so tied to romance, she decided not to get one. She didn't need the reminder of the thing that eluded her year after year. The idea of wearing the ring with the heart pointed out to show she was available wasn't her vibe. No point in advertising to the world she didn't have a boyfriend.

She waited for a couple to enter before exiting. A man held the outer door for her.

"Miss Knight?"

Dana registered the voice before she recognized Officer Worth out of uniform. Still handsome. "I didn't recognize you in clothes." Heat rushed to her face. "I mean…"

His laugh echoed in the narrow street. "I'm undercover as an American tourist. Did you find a ring?"

"Not really looking for one. I took advantage of the video to sit for a while."

"Hey, you don't have crutches today."

"No. I've been super conservative about using them. At home, I would have ditched them days ago."

He glanced up the street. "Where is the rest of your group?"

"On an excursion."

"They left you behind again?"

"No, this one was my choice not to go. I decided that hiking along the cliffs wasn't for me at the moment."

"Understandable. So what are you doing?"

"Window shopping mostly."

"Instead of hiking, you're walking all around Galway? You'll put on almost as many miles as you would on the cliffs."

"Yes, but I can go slowly and stop at every café. What are you doing off ship?" If he could ask about her, it was only fair she asked a few questions back.

"I need to purchase a Claddagh ring."

"Girlfriend in every port?"

"I see the video indoctrinated you."

"Maybe. I take it you've seen it before."

"I think it's required that everybody who comes to Galway learn about the ring."

Curiosity was killing her. Of course, he had a girlfriend, probably another crew member. Still, Dana wanted an answer to the question he'd sidestepped. "So, who is the special person who gets a ring from you?"

"My mother."

Unexpected. He didn't look like one of those men who spent a lot of time with his mother.

He cleared his throat. "Will you help me find the right one for her? I don't know much about jewelry."

Ring shopping? Weird, but it would be nice to spend some time with him. "Sure, do you know what she likes?"

"No. She wants something to replace her wedding and engagement ring while she goes through chemo."

"Your mother has cancer?"

"Yes. That's the reason this is my last cruise for a while. I'm taking a sabbatical to go home to be with her."

"Have you tried many stores?"

"This is the first one." He held the door for her again and they returned inside.

The traditional Claddagh ring with a crown on top of the heart held by two hands was an iconic symbol. Perhaps it was because she didn't wear many rings, but she found the traditional ring style not that engaging. The crown seemed like it would snag on sleeves. "Silver or gold, what does she like?"

Officer Worth shrugged.

"Do you know her size?"

"Seven."

"Same as me."

They looked at ring after ring, eliminating various styles. Officer Worth agreed that the versions with the larger crowns could easily catch on things.

"May I help you?" The saleswoman had a lilt to her voice.

"Yes," answered Officer Worth. "Can we try these two rings on? And I like the ones with the emerald hearts. Do you have any in US size seven?"

The saleswoman looked to Dana for confirmation, before bringing them to a less busy area of the counter.

While the woman pulled the rings out from under the counter, Dana looked at the selection under the glass. A non-traditional rose gold ring stood out. Not for the officer's mother, but for her.

The saleswoman set two black velvet boxes in front of Officer Worth. "Did something catch your eye, miss?"

Dana looked up. "Mine. No. We are looking for his mother."

The saleswoman winked at Officer Worth. "You should get one for your girlfriend, too."

"She's not—"

"He's not—"

Dana and Officer Worth's answers tumbled over each other.

He cleared his throat. "Miss Knight is just giving me a woman's opinion."

The saleswoman looked from one to another. "You aren't even on a first name basis?"

Dana inched away. Hoping that McKay would answer.

"It's complicated."

The saleswoman smiled. "It isn't as complicated as you think. Ireland is a magical place. Let me show you these rings."

McKay focused on the rings at the counter. He picked up the emerald heart one and twisted it in the light. "Miss Knight, er Dana," Although her name had been swimming through his mind, tasting it on his tongue felt intimate.

"Dana's fine."

"Would you try this one on? I want to see if I like it on a hand too."

Dana modeled it for him.

"I think my mother would like this the most."

"You said she wanted it for her chemo days. She might prefer the less expensive silver ones, so if she loses it, she won't feel as bad." Dana slipped the ring off and set it in front of McKay.

"Ach, I got just the thing." The saleswoman hurried to the end of the counter.

"I'm sorry if she embarrassed you with the girlfriend thing," he said.

Dana laughed. "It is a natural assumption. Two people about the same age shopping together for rings. Although I am not sure I should use your name or not."

"Off the ship, you may."

"How about I avoid using your name at all?"

The saleswoman returned with a selection of silver rings. "These are all under twenty and I'll give ye half off with the purchase of one of these others."

Was it his imagination or did the saleswoman's Irish brogue become heavier as she inched toward a sale?

"Dana, which one?"

"This one is almost exactly the same size and design as the emerald one. I suggest a matched pair." Dana pointed to the one in the middle of the selection.

McKay turned to the saleswoman. "They are both sevens in US ring sizes? Without my mother here—"

The woman produced a long metal wand and dropped first one ring then the other on it. "Yes, they both show as sevens."

"I'll get them both."

The saleswoman bustled about putting the velvet ring displays on the back counter and wrapping his chosen rings. Dana stayed by his side, looking at the other rings on display.

He leaned closer and spoke so the saleswoman wouldn't hear. "I am curious. Which ring do you keep looking at?"

Dana tapped the glass. "The rose gold one, third one down."

"You should try it on."

"What is the point? I am not buying one."

The saleswoman returned with McKay's purchase and his tax-free card. "You should try it on, miss. You never know."

"I'm afraid I'll love it, and it isn't in my price range. But thank you." Dana smiled at the saleswoman and exited the store.

McKay followed after her. "Thanks for your help. What are your plans for the rest of the day?"

"Purchase a sweater. I found one I like but I want to make sure there isn't one I like better. Then there is a hop-on bus tour with a stop at the top of the street. I figure I can ride it around and see the rest of the town. When I'm done, it stops closer to the dock."

"Do you mind if I tag along while you shop? I need to get my sister and my niece something."

They wandered up the street in and out of crowded shops.

"McKay," Dana called to get his attention. "Look at this sheep. Would your niece like him? He is the cutest of the ones I've seen today."

McKay picked up the stuffed animal, surprised to see it was made in Ireland with real Irish wool and not halfway across the globe. "I think Gracie will love it."

Dana picked up three smaller versions of the sheep. "Definitely a kid pleaser."

"Who are those for? Nieces and nephews?"

Dana laughed. "Cheyanne is my only sibling, not an aunt yet. These are work related."

"So, you can't tell me, or you have to—?"

"Never speak with you again, among other things." Dana paid for her purchases and waited for him.

He waved to the top of the street. "Only a couple of stores left. Have you found a sweater better than the first one you saw?"

"No."

"You should go back and get it, then. You don't want it to be the one that got away."

"You're right."

They backtracked to a side street and entered the shop. Dana went straight to the sweater she liked, a traditional pattern in blue. A lavender one in a similar style sat next to it.

"Wow, I think you found my sister's sweater, too." McKay looked at the tag. "I'm never sure if I should get a medium or a large."

"What size does she say she wears?"

"Sometimes both."

"Then err on the side of too large for a sweater like this. She can always wear it over another shirt."

He stood behind her in line. "I'm glad I ran into you today. I don't think I would have found the right gifts without some help."

"I'm surprised you didn't find a crew member to help you shop."

McKay smiled and didn't reply. Explaining his dating availability status was not a subject to share with an acquaintance, especially one he would date if he could. He gestured to the cafe across the street. "Would you like ice cream? My treat for keeping you standing so long."

Dana bit her lip. "Is that allowed? I wouldn't want you in trouble for involvement with a passenger."

"It is an outdoor table. When we finish, you can walk up to the bus kiosk, and I'll go back to the ship. A simple thank you. Very public. Nothing illicit." If that wasn't a justification, he wasn't sure what was. He'd tell Alvaro as soon as he returned. Better to self-report that nothing happened than have another crew member see them and make assumptions.

"Only because I need to sit." Dana sat at the closest empty table and looked at the line, waiting to make a purchase. "I should have gotten my ice cream first."

"What flavor do you want? I'll get it while you watch the bags. If that isn't a problem."

"I can watch bags. They are hardly likely to do anything requiring my expertise."

He chuckled. "I forgot, personal security, watching bags should be easy. I'm more worried about anyone who tries to take them now."

"They won't get that far. Chocolate based anything."

The answer to his flavor question brought him back from picturing her taking out would be thieves. "Cone or cup?"

"Cone, of course."

All too soon, they finished their cones, and Dana waved goodbye as she crossed the street to the bus kiosk.

McKay rose and walked the other direction. If only he could keep this encounter to himself. However, the best course was to report it. If he didn't, it was unlikely that he would be reprimanded, since it was his last week and there had been no physical contact. As tempting as it was to skirt the rules, he wouldn't, he couldn't. He neared the jewelry store where he'd run into Dana. Through the window, he watched the saleswoman sell rings to another customer. If only her mistake had been right, and Dana was his girlfriend—he'd have done something impulsive.

Nine

She'd overdone it in Galway. Dana tightened the wrap on her ankle. She used the room phone to call room service and request ice. Then she dialed guest services to cancel her ticket on tomorrow's excursion to the castle.

As she hung up the phone, she realized she was tearing up. Not from pain. Frustration.

The castle excursion was the only one she had booked for herself. It wasn't part of Cheyanne's group plans.

Stupid romance books. Viscounts, dukes, milk maids, princesses in castles, and knights in shining armor. Fairy tales in Irish castles didn't happen, so she shouldn't be crying. Right? The tears came harder. Wiping her eyes, Dana opened her calendar app on her phone. Maybe this was a bad case of PMS. Crying over missing a castle was ridiculous.

A knock came on her door. Ice.

Dana hobbled to answer.

Juan stood there with a bucket. He looked at her face. "Do you need anything else? The ship has a doctor if—"

"Thanks, Juan. Ice is all I need. I just overdid it." She was about to close the door when her sister came bouncing up the hallway.

"Dana! There you are. I've been texting."

Juan waved as he left.

"I'm sorry. My phone must not be receiving them." Or she hadn't wanted to check. Dana opened the door further and stepped back to let her sister in.

"Ice? Does it hurt again? Is that why you're crying?"

Dana sat on the bed so she could prepare her ice pack. "What were you texting me about?"

Cheyanne wagged her finger. "You don't get to sidestep my questions that easily?"

"I'm going to try. How was your day?" Dana set the ice pack on her ankle.

"Better than yours apparently. Did you injure it again?" Cheyanne sat on the bed.

"No. I just overestimated what I could do."

"And that has you crying? You let me come to the gym with you when you spar those Hastings guys and take some pretty hard hits. And I haven't seen you cry over your ankle once. Is it worse than you let on?"

"No, I'll be fine for your wedding. It doesn't hurt much at all, only like a four."

"But you are crying."

Dana blinked back more tears. "Just PMS."

"Fine, don't tell me the real reason. Anyway, I was texting you to come to dinner in our suite tonight. I ordered extra huge portions, then we are getting in the hot tub."

"I was thinking of ordering room service so I could just stay here."

"In this cave?"

Dana looked at the one white wall. "It is rather cave-like."

"And sitting in here with a cheese sandwich, or whatever you order, and your PMS is only going to make it worse. Grab your crutches and come up to the suite. It is a girls only night. No mom. And we all understand PMS."

"Will there be chocolate?"

"Of course. What is a girls' night without chocolate?"

"Can we wait for fifteen minutes? I don't want to haul the ice pack all over the ship."

"No problem. Do you want your swimsuit? I can get it while you sit."

"It is in the second drawer." Dana pointed to the closet area.

"What did you do that stressed your ankle?"

"Shopped."

"I want to see."

"Hand me that bag. I stuffed everything inside."

Cheyanne grabbed the bag off the desk where Dana had dropped it earlier. "Oh, I love this sweater. I didn't even think of buying one. I really should. Did you know Ireland is famous for its sheep?"

A laugh bubbled out of Dana's mouth. "And here I thought they just liked wool sweaters and the white dots on the hills were cotton balls."

"Don't laugh at me." Cheyanne held the sweater up and looked in the mirror. "The lighting in here is awful. Still, the sweater would look great on me."

"Not. It is for me to wear in Chicago winters, not for you to wear in England."

"Can't blame me for trying. I'll have to shop at our next port." The paper bag crunched as Cheyanne rummaged through it. "Chocolate?"

"Don't you dare open them. They are gifts for my friends. Some-one," *McKay*, "told me Irish Cadbury is made with Irish milk. Some say it is better than UK Cadbury. I am going to buy the same bars in London and have a taste test party when I get home."

"Invite me."

"I think you are supposed to be on your honeymoon and then settling into your new home in the UK."

"Options, options. Marriage. Chocolate party." Cheyanne balanced imaginary weights in her hands. "I guess I'll have to pass on the party."

"I'm sure you'll get plenty of chocolate living here."

"I'm not sure of that. On our excursion, we stopped at a restaurant. And we had Sticky Toffee pudding. So good. Then Chandler reminded me if I ate too much, I wouldn't fit in my dress. I wanted to slap him. I worked out for an hour with him in the gym this morning and hiked on the excursion."

"That wasn't nice."

Cheyanne set the bag on the bed and plopped down. "It may only be pre-wedding jitters, but Chandler has been odd this entire cruise. It is like Mom is rubbing off on him. He didn't like the way I got my nails done on spa day, my brand of sunscreen, and last night when we were dancing, he kept correcting me. It wasn't like we were doing ballroom or anything. Just normal dancing. Tell me I am imagining things."

Not the conversation Dana wanted with her sister. Chandler had always been condescending to her and joked about her nanny status. However, he made her sister happy. "Has anything else changed?"

"You are going to think I'm stupid." Chey sniffed one of the chocolate bars. "His kisses are, well, not as passionate. It feels like he is kissing me out of duty. I thought I'd see more of him on the cruise, too."

Dana leaned against the wall so she could see her sister better. "I thought you both planned activities away from each other."

"Like tonight's impromptu ladies' night because he decided he wanted more time with his groomsmen to play that roleplaying game?"

Dana glanced at the pink paper tacked above the desk. "That's right, tonight was supposed to be another restaurant and a show."

"I don't mind much, as this gives me an excuse to ditch Mom. Don't ask her on your bachelorette excursion."

"Wasn't planning to. I may invite her the day before my wedding as a guest. Then I won't be disappointed when she can't come."

"I should have done that." Chey toyed with the bag.

"She would have never forgiven you. I have nothing to lose. I am already in the never-forgive box for calling Child Protection Services on myself and then going to court to have custody changed. You don't want to be there with me." As much counseling as Dana attended, her mother's rejection still hurt.

"Wait what? I know about the court thing, but CPS?"

"In my defense I was nine, so you were three-ish? Although their home inspection didn't show signs of any physical abuse or outright neglect. The report was used in court to show the unequal treatment of her children which my advocate argued was emotional abuse. Mom is never going to forgive me." The ice pack grew soft as the ice melted and Dana adjusted where it was positioned.

Cheyanne pulled three pairs of shamrock socks out of the bag. "These are cute."

"More gifts for friends. Wait until you see the little sheep. They are the best."

Opening the bag as wide as possible, Cheyanne peered in. "How small are they?"

"The size of your hand."

"There aren't any sheep in here." Her sister dumped the bag on the bed next to her.

No sheep.

"There has to be. I bought them for the Ogilvie kids. Even if their parents can buy them all of Ireland, I wanted to bring them a gift, so they know I care."

"Sorry sis. Your three little wards—"

"Principals."

"Little kids shouldn't have that title. But anyway, there are no sheep here."

Dana leaned back against the wall. "I must have left them at the cafe. We were talking, and I had to hurry to not miss the bus."

"Who is we?"

"Just a guy."

"Maybe he has them. Is he a passenger?"

Dana hated misleading her sister, but it would be worse if her sister knew about McKay. "No, he isn't."

"You're telling me that you had ice cream with some stranger you met in Galway?"

"Something like that."

"He must have had one beauty of an accent for you to do that."

Dana smiled, desperate to change the subject. "It looks like my ice is done. Shall we go?"

"At least tell me you got a photo of the mystery sheep thief."

"Nope."

"A phone number."

"Nope."

"I can't believe this. My sister, the bodyguard, had ice cream with a random guy in Ireland and has no evidence. What about a receipt?"

"He paid."

Chey groaned and opened the door so they could leave. "You owe me more details. Was he a ginger? Was he handsome?"

"No, and yes." Dana checked that the door shut and was locked.

"Can you be less mysterious? I've already had it with Erin sneaking off all the time to see someone for a shipboard romance. Amy-Kate is just as bad having to go out for air. I told her to get seasick patches."

Dana pushed the elevator button. "Well you don't have to worry about me. No shipboard romance." Throughout the evening Dana alternated between wondering if McKay had her sheep and wishing that she could start a shipboard romance.

Another day down. The ten-day cruise was half over. McKay signed out of his computer and turned it over to the night officer.

"Anything to be aware of?" asked Martina.

McKay scrolled through the electronic log. "A passenger who discovered the blind spot between cameras 9-045 and 047. He used it two nights ago and again tonight. If I hadn't been watching, I wouldn't have noticed. Our walk-by has moved him and the woman he is with down the hall, but anyone who finds a blind spot and keeps using it is a red flag."

"Do we know who he is?"

"Chandler Fairfax, of the UK."

"Isn't he the groom in that big wedding party?"

"Yup."

"And I take it he wasn't with the bride." Martina settled into her seat at the monitor.

"Nope."

"Yikes. I feel bad for the woman he is marrying."

"Same. I wish I could come up with a reason for her to go down that hallway at the right time. But the bride is in the Diamond Suite and she is unlikely to go on deck eleven for any reason."

Martina sat in the chair and logged in. "Hmmm. If it is quiet tonight, I'll look at the footage and try to see if he has been there more than twice. Maybe we can come up with ideas that don't break any privacy rules. I want to save the bride some trouble."

"Careful Martina, our hands are tied." Even having the connection with Dana, he couldn't think of a way to let Cheyanne know about her unfaithful man.

"I know. And I won't do anything without Alvaro's approval."

"I want to know how he found out about that spot. I can't think of a way he could have other than bribing a crew member. That is a security risk."

"Is he with the same woman each time?"

"Yes, a redhead. I've narrowed her down to seven possibilities, including two bridesmaids."

"Ew. Worse and worse." Martina tapped a pen on the desk. "But she could have done the bribing."

"I hadn't thought of that."

"Women can be devious too."

"Let me know if you think of something. We need to find out how they learned about that spot." That was a security risk he could act on.

"Will do. Good night."

The door to Alvaro's office stood open. His boss waved him in and pointed to his tablet. "What is this?"

McKay entered and sat down. "I thought my report was self-explanatory."

"You reported yourself for talking to a passenger."

"I treated her to ice cream."

"You know as well as I do it does not fall into the relations category."

"But I wanted to hold her hand. I want to see her again. So, I am turning myself in to prevent me from doing anything stupid."

"I've known you for years. I've watched women, passengers, and crew throw themselves at you and even stalk you. You have never even come close to crossing lines."

"I've never wanted to."

"So, you want to now?"

"I have no desire to dishonor my position. But I do want to get to know Dana Knight better."

"Is she aware of the cruise line policy?"

"Yes. She even brought it up today when we were at the cafe."

Alvaro sighed. "I'm deleting this report. There is no reason for it to go on your record, especially if you want to be rehired."

"But—"

"No buts. If anyone else on this ship turned in a report like this, would we keep it?"

"No. But I am not anyone else. I am an officer. I am held to a higher standard."

"You didn't even hold hands."

"No, but I wanted to."

Alvaro ran his hand over his salt and pepper hair. "So you are preemptively turning this in so you won't need to turn in a real one?"

"Something like that."

"Noted. Deleted. Talk to Miss Knight as much as you want to in the public areas. Don't use security resources to locate her. Is that what you needed to hear?"

"I just needed someone else to be aware so I would be accountable."

"Done. Good night." With his dismissal, Alvaro turned his attention back to the tablet.

McKay checked the time. He had an hour before his nightly phone call to his sister. As much as he wanted to go searching the decks for Dana, it wasn't a wise move at the moment. He needed to figure out how to deal with Chandler Fairfax and the redhead or he might say something to Dana he shouldn't.

He walked down the corridor and stood in the blind spot, looking for inspiration. Without proof of a crime, there was nothing they could do. Judging from the passionate kiss, the elevator camera captured the redhead, whom he recognized from the wedding party, seemed very willing to be with Mr. Fairfax. The suspicion that Mr. Fairfax or the redhead were not enough to act upon. But if they were right, and someone purchased the information with evil intent—assault on board was not taken lightly. If he could prevent even one, he would. A couple returning to their cabin prompted him to move on.

Once in his cabin, McKay shed his uniform and put it on a hanger with a laundry tag. He double checked the pockets.

The bags from his shopping trip sat on the bed waiting for him to find a place in his already crowded luggage for them. The jewelry store purchase went into an inner pocket of his backpack. Better to keep that with him on the plane. The sweater for Jen found a spot in his suitcase, filling the last corner. He had yet to pack the last of his civilian clothing.

There was no helping it. He would need to check a third bag to go home. How had he gathered so much stuff in the last six months? He refolded a Cancun t-shirt. It was two years old. Since he hadn't renegotiated his next contract, there wasn't an option to leave his personal items in company storage. When he came back, he'd need to remember to cull his ever-increasing T-shirt collection or start collecting postcards.

He'd leave Gracie's sheep in its bag until he found a space for it.

His phone rang.

Jen's face appeared on the screen. She was sitting in her car. "Sorry for calling early. I got called into work and I am taking Gracie to Mom's."

"Is Mom up to that?"

"I hope so." Jen handed the phone to the back seat.

Gracie's face appeared on the screen. "I'm gonna be very good. I get to take your music." Her voice lowered to a whisper. "I will try not to talk too much, but it is so hard not to tell Grandma all the things."

"Save some things to tell her tomorrow." McKay hoped his advice would work.

Lights of passing cars illuminated Gracie's face. "I'll be good. I know Grandma is sick and is tired like I used to be, before my new heart."

McKay tamped down his emotions. As much as they all tried to treat Gracie like a normal kid, his niece understood sickness, hospitals, and death better than most people three times her age. "Did your mom tell you about counting sheep?"

"I read a book about counting sheep. It's silly."

"I didn't understand it either until I saw all the sheep on a farm in Ireland."

"Is that the one where you saw the dogs?" Gracie referred to a conversation over a month ago, the first time he'd sailed around the Emerald Isle.

"Yes. From the ship you can see the hills are covered with white dots." McKay reached into the bag to show her the lamb he bought. His hand closed around two lambs. "One second, I need to put my phone down."

Gracie chattered about the videos he'd sent of the sheep dogs while McKay looked in the shopping bag. Four stuffed sheep, one large and three small, lay in a tangle. One of the small sheep looked up at him with large plastic eyes as if asking him why he wasn't with his owner. Quickly, he extracted the largest of the stuffed animals and picked up his phone.

Gracie was just finishing her monologue. "…anyway, mom *still* says I can't have a dog. Can I have a sheep? Then I can really count them."

Jen laughed, now sharing the screen with her daughter and obviously in his mother's driveway. "No. Sheep are more work than dogs."

"That's a problem…" McKay rubbed his chin, getting both his sister's and niece's attention.

The wrinkle above Jen's brow deepened, Gracie's eyes widened.

He held up the stuffed animal. "I got this sheep for Gracie."

Gracie let out a little yell of delight. "Uncle Mac, you got me a sheep?"

"Yes, and when he can't sleep, e counts little girls." He wiggled the stuffed animal.

"That's silly."

"I don't know. Maybe you can try it at Grandma's. You count sheep and he can count girls and see who falls asleep faster."

"He is a stuffed animal and he can't sleep."

"Or he is always sleeping."

"If I get out of bed and bug Grandma, I won't get him, will I?"

Oops. He hadn't seen that one coming.

Jen must have noticed his surprise and answered. "Uncle Mac will still give it to you, but it may have to stay in time out for a while."

Gracie pinched her lips together and nodded.

McKay scrambled for a change in subject. "You can also count how many hours until I get home."

"How many is that?"

"I am not sure. Less than 240." Easy math. He'd be home in less than ten days, even if there were multiple plane delays.

"That is a lot of hours." Gracie wasn't wrong. In hours, it sounded longer.

Jen took control of the phone. "We need to go in now. Have a good night, Mac."

"Tell mom, I love her. I won't add to the chaos by calling." He waved. "Night Gracie. Sleep well."

The phone call ended. He dumped out the bag holding Dana's sheep. How had that mix up happened and how could he get them back to her? She said she was going on a shore excursion tomorrow, didn't she? When she came back on ship he would tell her that he had them. He was already assigned to work that shift. No stalking of her location necessary. He'd just catch her when she came on board.

Ten

A WHITE ENVELOPE WITH THE cruise ship logo hung from the
clip on Dana's door. Probably the excursion ticket for the castle
she'd had to cancel. She took it off and folded it into her pocket
and continued on to breakfast. The ship had docked in the pre-
dawn hours and passengers were already making their way off
the ship into the little town of Killybegs for their excursions.
Despite the exodus, the buffet room was full. Dana grabbed
a light breakfast, including the day's special, crepes with berries.

She found a seat by the window where she could look at the
village built on the side of the green hills surrounding the harbor.
A gentle rain fell, shrouding Killybegs in an ethereal mist. Possibilities of fairies and leprechauns surrounded the town. Dana
longed to explore, to see if she could find a sparkle of magic
for herself.

The ship's daily newsletter said the town's population was less
than the number of crew onboard, so the town wasn't that large.
If she walked slowly on the steep hill, she'd be safe enough. And
unlike the castle tour she'd given up, people would not need to
wait for her to make the steep ascent. Or she could keep her
original plan and read in the ship's library for the day. Her book
sounded less appealing.

Looking out the window, she paid less attention to the food than she should have and a berry fell off her fork and bounced off her shirt, leaving a dot of dark red syrup. She dabbed it off the best she could and reached for another napkin. The envelope in her pocket crinkled. She'd forgotten about it. After finishing her crepe—which was yummy enough she didn't entirely regret the ruined shirt—Dana opened the envelope. It wasn't an excursion ticket. Instead, it was two folded papers.

Dana Knight,

We are very sorry for the inconvenience, however, because of a maintenance issue we need to move you to another cabin before sailing time today. We hope that moving you to a balcony suite will make up for any disruption in your trip. Your new room will be on deck 11...

A scribble of blue ink obliterated the printed name of the Chief Purser who signed the letter.

The other paper was directions on how to contact her room steward to move her belongings, etc. Dana read the message a second time. A balcony? Maybe she didn't need to leave the ship to find a bit of Irish magic after all.

She sipped the last of her juice. Pale rays of sun penetrated the space between clouds. Dana folded the letter up and looked out the window. The town called to her. She couldn't let this chance slip by to make a memory. A slow walk around town while the room steward moved her room, seemed like just the thing. As soon as she changed her shirt, of course.

Martina's plan was simple: move Dana to a cabin near the blind spot on deck eleven. Because of an electrical problem, the ship had sailed with several empty cabins, including one just two doors down from the blind spot. Yesterday, after a replacement part arrived at the Galway port, maintenance completed the cabin repairs. If Dana moved to the newly repaired cabin, with a bit of luck, either Dana or her sister would catch the fiancé and cause enough noise that security could intervene. Then they could question Chandler Fairfax and his red-haired friend about their choice of location for the clandestine meetings.

McKay hated the plan.

They overruled his vote. He was all for someone telling the bride she might want to rethink her wedding plans and even giving Dana a room upgrade. However, putting Dana in the awkward position of having to tell her sister about the infidelity, not so much. Or worse, if Dana discovered the couple and a fight ensued, she could be hurt. Although being a Hastings employee, it was more likely she would inflict well deserved pain on Mr. Fairfax. Which could lead to Dana's removal from the ship.

The real problem was that the only way this plan would accomplish the true goal of finding out which crew member had leaked the blind spot location required the bride to blow up at the groom in such a way that crew members became involved. They needed to orchestrate a confrontation, if possible.

Deception.

With Dana in the middle of it.

Why not add a camera to remove the dead spot? His suggestion was met with the same explanation security gave when the extra cameras were installed: The ship's electrical system didn't have the capacity at some points. Dead spots were unavoidable. Most of the spots were smaller than a meter. Blah, blah, blah. This dead spot was the largest one in the passenger area due to a jog in the hallway.

Frustration mounting, McKay paced the corridor, searching for an alternative solution. His phone buzzed with a message from Alvaro summoning him to the security chief's office.

His boss didn't glance up from his computer as McKay entered. "Shut the door and have a seat."

McKay complied, settling in to wait while Alvaro collected his thoughts.

Alvaro broke the silence. "I know you disapprove of Martina's scheme. I wanted to explain why I green-lit it. The leak about that blind spot must have come from this department, either directly or through a lower-ranking crew member. I like your idea of an off-network camera. I've put one on hold at a shop in Belfast. The trip should take you about five and a half hours."

"Where am I going to get a car? Passengers have rented everything within miles." McKay didn't mention that the last time he drove on the left side of the road, it hadn't gone well.

"I asked the port authority to arrange something. You better go change. You'll be far too conspicuous in your uniform. Get off with the crew going ashore. It will cut into your scheduled work time a bit, but I'll cover for you."

"You don't think it will seem odd to the rest of the crew that I won't be at my post when passengers return?"

"Fortuitous timing, since this is your last voyage for a while, I'll say I approved extra leave, so no one should be suspicious." Alvaro's eyes gleamed with sly humor. "Stop by a tourist shop and pick up an Irish souvenir while you're out."

"I've already added one extra suitcase to my flight home."

"Get something small, then. Something you can put the camera in, since you will still need to go through security. Crew is looking for food and weapons. It shouldn't be hard."

"The head of security is telling me to bypass security protocols."

"Yes." Alvaro's grin widened. "First time for everything."

"That should be interesting."

Interesting was not the right word for the rest of his day.

The Port Authority's niece and her best friend—both university students—were off for the summer. According to them, they had nothing better to do than to drive a *dathúil* American to Belfast.

Their tiny VW Polo belonged in a circus. At six-foot-three, McKay had to fold himself practically in half to fit, his knees jammed against the dash and his elbow kept banging against the door. If he had to guess, he'd say the car was older than he was. Clearly, Volkswagen hadn't had men of his stature in mind when they designed this model. McKay learned more about Irish music in the two-and-a-half-hour drive into Belfast than could be squeezed into a semester-long class. Occasionally, the women burst into fits of laughter when speaking in their native tongue. McKay couldn't understand them, but he knew it involved him.

The electronics store he needed was located in a large shopping center. The women gave him a half hour to find what he needed and meet them back at the entrance. The store employee tried to up-sell him on a camera hidden in a Guinness bottle. It might be useful for someone who was guarding the contents of their refrigerator, not so much for ship security.

A few shops down, he found a souvenir store full of kitschy items made on the other side of the world. A leprechaun flashlight presented as the best item to sneak a tiny camera onboard in. Unless security examined it closely during the x-ray scan, they'd likely overlook it.

On the return trip, McKay kept his eyes glued to his watch, studiously ignoring the speedometer. Plausible deniability seemed the wisest course when it came to the velocity at which the car whipped along the narrow roads.

The Polo shuddered as the niece turned into the pier yard just as the security team was wrapping up the boarding process. McKay hoped his absence and near late arrive didn't cause too much of a stir.

"Cutting it a bit close there, Mac," Martina remarked as he approached the checkpoint.

"Would you believe I lost track of time?"

"This port of call is the smallest one on this cruise, so no. I thought you'd at least be out with someone…" Ian, one of the greener team members, raised a suggestive eyebrow. The newest member of the security team had broken more than one crew member's heart. During the last cruise, McKay had tried to get the newbie to focus less on romancing and more on work. Ian seemed intent on flirting with every female crew member onboard.

McKay set his things down on the conveyor belt feeding the scanner. He kept up the conversation to distract his coworkers. "Why, did you guys have a bet on where I'd gone?"

"One of the guys from the kitchen said he saw you take off in a car with two women. I told him it must be a rideshare. You aren't the type to take off with two local girls for the day." Martina didn't even look at the screen as his belongings passed through. He'd need to make a note for Alvaro to remind security staff not to automatically trust crew members even if they knew them well.

"Rideshare." Not exactly a lie. "I'd better go throw myself on Alvaro's mercy before he cuts me loose." McKay grabbed his bags off the belt, eager to escape.

Ian laughed. "You are his favorite, the golden boy. And with only a few days left, who wants to do the paperwork?"

McKay forced a chuckle as he beat a hasty retreat.

As he wove his way through the ship toward his cabin, McKay's thoughts drifted back to Dana. Much as it pained him, using her as bait might be their best shot at drawing out their mole. He just hoped she could forgive him for putting her in such an uncomfortable position.

Balcony.

One single word could entirely change a cruise. Magic had happened in the mists. The window, the view; it was truly amazing. Some sprite had worked overtime.

Dana could get used to this life all too easily. No wandering around the ship searching for a comfortable place to sit while reading. No overhearing conversations she wanted no part of. No worries that Sheila would sneak up on her.

And sunlight! Or the enchanting gray fog of a misty morning.

And towel animals.

She'd returned after dinner to find a towel dog in the middle of her bed surrounded by her missing sheep. A cabin steward must have found them when they cleaned her old room. Odd, she'd checked everywhere, even under the bed before leaving. She took photos of the creation to send to Brit, Simone, and Dad.

If she'd had this room from the start, she might not have left it for most of the cruise. She almost wished she hadn't agreed to meet her sister and the other bridesmaids at the evening show. Reading her latest historical romance and listening to the sea was much more appealing.

Dana closed her eBook app and stretched. She'd never thought of herself as much of an introvert, but the last few days on the ship she'd discovered how much she enjoyed solitary time. Now that she had a room with a view, she wished for another at-sea-day, or two. But the pink paper called. Tonight, the magic show.

Dana brushed her teeth and reapplied her makeup. She couldn't put this off any longer. Time to go.

It wasn't hard to find the bridal party once she neared the theater. Just follow the giggling.

"Dana?" Cheyanne jumped up and down and waved an arm. "I stopped by your room earlier, but I didn't catch you."

"Which one?"

"What do you mean, which one? The one I always stop at."

"Oh," her sister must not have gotten her text message. "There was an electrical issue, so they moved me to a new room."

"That is inconvenient."

"Not bad actually, the room came with a balcony. Cruising got a hundred times better with that."

"I know what you mean. The suite we are in has spoiled me for anything less."

The line into the theater surged forward as the doors opened. Dana sat between her sister and Amy-Kate. The magic show was much better than Dana expected, and all the bridesmaids were in good humor. Erin and Renee spent the time giggling over someone they'd met. Lindie sat on the far side of the group, clapping the loudest.

The final curtain fell. As they were leaving, her mother approached. Dana broke off from the group so as not to ruin the mood.

"Where are your crutches?"

"I don't need them anymore."

"I thought you were going to stay on them and make sure you didn't ruin Cheyanne's wedding."

"I stayed on them longer than I would at home. I am being careful."

"You could have fallen and ruined your sister's wedding. I saw you wandering about town today with that steep hill. It is practically a cliff."

Dana had passed a woman on a knee scooter going to the cathedral, it wasn't *that* steep. "A short walk. No harm."

"No harm? You are trying to ruin my wedding." Sheila's voice rose.

Her wedding? That would be a shock to Chandler. That and a herd of other snappy comebacks raced through Dana's mind. "I'm being very careful not to do that."

Cheyanne joined them. She touched their mother on the shoulder. "Mom, Dana is trying. She even gave up going to a castle today. Lay off, ok?"

Sheila snorted and turned away.

"Come on Dana, Chandler is meeting us in the bar." Cheyanne's statement wasn't as much of an invitation as it was a direction.

Without the crutches, Dana didn't have a good excuse to skip joining in. The bar would serve her an overpriced bottle of water or a carbonated drink as easily as anywhere else. Dana followed as the women navigated to the other end of the ship and up three levels.

The bar was surprisingly cozy. Plush seats and couches were arranged in comfortable groupings around the room. Chandler and the groomsmen claimed a section in the corner.

"About time, Luv." Chandler pulled Cheyanne into his lap and locked his lips with hers.

Cheyanne squealed and tried to get up. "Not here."

"I hardly get to see you. And I haven't had a good kiss in hours."

"That is the point of a bachelorette cruise." Amy-Kate sat in the vacant seat next to Chandler. "Not seeing the man you are going to spend the rest of your life with for a week."

A groomsman stood with his drink, allowing Dana to take a seat. "Wonkiest bachelorette I've ever been to, and with the bride's parents no less. It's like being on a high school trip with chaperones running all over."

"Have you ever been to a bachelorette before?" asked Dana.

"No. But I've imagined them. There was more drinking…" He gave her a crooked smile.

Dana put up her hand. "I don't think I want to know."

"You are the one that doesn't drink, right?" asked another groomsman.

"Correct."

"What is up with that? Are you in AA or something?" This one spoke in a decidedly American accent, Ron, if she remembered right.

Dana hated this part. Why did people need to defend their choice to not drink? It should be normalized by now. If someone needed AA, it was Ron. She had yet to see him without a drink in his hand. Maybe she should point out that the "Friends of Bill W." meetups in the cruise newsletters were for Alcoholics Anonymous.

"I like to keep my hands free in case I need to throw the first punch."

Another grooms-minion snapped his fingers. "That's right, you're a bodyguard. Right? Apparently, they are an equal opportunity thing."

Dana ignored the comment. Her superpower was that she wasn't what she appeared to be. If she looked like a supermodel weight lifter, she wouldn't blend in."

"But you aren't at work." Ron leaned closer.

"Yet, I still don't want a drink." Even water. Dana hoped he'd turn his attention elsewhere. She wasn't in the mood to fend off unwanted passes.

Ron sat on the arm of her chair, his voice dropped to a husky whisper. "You'd be hot if you weren't so uptight."

Uptight? Who used words like that? Dana didn't bother hiding her eye roll. "If you are trying to flirt, you are failing."

His hand dropped on her shoulder and drifted downward.

Dana slid her thumb under his hand, lifting it off with a twist.

Ron jumped up, shaking his hand. "You —"

"Is there a problem here?"

Dana hadn't noticed the security officer behind them, but she recognized the voice instantly.

"That—" Under McKay's glare, Ron apparently thought better of whatever name he wished to call her. "She broke my hand."

"Miss?" McKay kept a straight face, but his eyes twinkled under raised brows.

"I removed his hand from my person as I do not consent to his advances. I assure you nothing is broken." She hadn't needed to apply that much pressure and she would have felt something break.

McKay turned to Ron. "From what I saw, she was defending herself. I'm sure the CCTV feed will agree with me. If you would like, I can call the ship's doctor to his office to see you or ask the bartender to give you some ice."

"That won't be necessary." Ron folded his arms, hiding the injured hand.

McKay walked off.

Everyone in their group stared at her. As well as people from neighboring sections. Poor Chey. Her sister didn't deserve this kind of attention. Dana stood. "Have fun, guys. I think it is best that I leave."

"So soon?" asked Cheyanne. "Ron was out of line and he knows it, right?"

"Good riddance," muttered one of the other grooms-minions.

Dana sent a silent prayer that Ron wasn't the one she was paired with for the wedding processional.

"I'm a bit tired." It wasn't a lie. The couch in her new suite was calling to her and her book. The heroine was about to make her grand gesture by climbing out the window to save the viscount's reputation. "Have a good night."

As Dana exited the bar, she felt a presence behind her. She turned. McKay. "Officer Worth, you don't need to follow me. I want to leave."

"That was an interesting move you used on that guy." He fell into step with her.

"Instinct. I should have pushed him away or something else."

"How do you like your new suite?"

"How do you — Never mind, of course, you know. It's very nice. You didn't have anything to do with that, did you?"

"Did you get your sheep back? I found them in my things."

He evaded. Why would he do that unless he did have something to do with the upgrade? She hadn't noticed an electrical problem. If ships were like buildings, a grid could include several unaffected rooms. She'd looked at enough floor plans on details to know that. Even so, his evasion was something to note.

"I wondered if the room steward found them. You need to see this." Dana opened her phone to the photo she'd taken of the dog watching over the sheep.

McKay laughed. "Wow. Looks like I owe someone a tip for that one. I'm glad you got them back."

"Why didn't you drop them by?" She knew the answer before she finished the question. What about McKay made her thinking muddled?

"Appearances. If someone saw me going to your suite—"

"Of course, I understand."

They'd reached the elevator. Dana pushed the button.

"Good evening," McKay turned to leave, then paused. "The guy deserved what you did. Don't feel bad about it."

The elevator door opened, and a passenger exited. Three others remained in the elevator.

Not wanting anyone to get the wrong idea, Dana nodded slightly at McKay as she entered the elevator. As the door closed, she caught one last glance of him. Why did she always want what she couldn't have? Right now, she would rather have a nice long conversation with him than to be curled up with her book no matter how grand of a gesture Miss Philipa made for her viscount. It didn't beat a conversation with a real-life man.

Eleven

Since McKay "officially" spent the day on leave, he had to work a night shift. Alvaro failed to mention the extra shift when he gave McKay the assignment to get the camera. McKay would have still agreed, but the extra hours were going to be hard to keep. Since Martina had worked a portion of his day shift, it was only fair that he work hers. If Alvaro was right, and a security team member was involved, any other work solution would be out of the ordinary. Not for the first time, McKay wished the ship served Dr. Pepper. In the end caffeine was caffeine, so he guzzled the ship's cola of choice as he monitored the new camera through Alvaro's tablet. Nothing unusual.

McKay covered a yawn. His body rebelled against being awake at two in the morning. The ship was quiet this time of night, with most of the activity happening in the casino where gamblers played round the clock, heedless of time or location.

He stood more to keep himself awake than anything. In the other room, two crew members monitored the CCTV feeds.

"Anything to report?"

"Nothing of import. A passenger left their power scooter in the hallway again. This will be their third warning."

"Too bad we don't have boots like they do for cars parked in the wrong zones," said Ian.

"Wouldn't solve the problem. It would still be in the hall," said a crew member McKay rarely saw as they worked opposite shifts.

"An impound lot. We'll tow it to the luggage area on deck 3." Ian had a point.

McKay brought up the feed of the scooter on his tablet, then crosschecked with the cabin information. "It is a rental with our contracted company. The passenger signed the acknowledgement. I also show they had two verbal warnings from housekeeping. Who wants to play tow truck? We have a master key."

"You're serious? We can do that?" Ian turned to face him. Three months on board, Ian should have known the policy by now.

"Yes. Usually people stop after one warning. It's been at least three sailings since the last time we had to take drastic steps. The cruise line has an arrangement with the rental company, so we can impound it for the rest of the trip."

"Wow, Mac. I didn't know you had a fierce side," Ian stood. "May I have the honors? I delivered the first warning, and the woman was a first-class Karen."

"Sure. I'll print out the letter explaining that they are in violation of the agreement with the ship and the rental company." It was petty, and if he had more sleep, he might have waited until morning. However, it was a fire hazard, so he felt justified. In the back of his mind, he knew the lingering annoyance with the groomsman that had bothered Dana fueled his actions.

By the time 0500 rolled around, McKay was ready to prop his eyes open with toothpicks.

Alvaro entered the office. He laughed at McKay's report of impounding the scooter. "I get to deal with an annoyed passenger as your payback for having you work a double?"

McKay made a show of looking at his watch. "I predict they'll be down by 0700 demanding their scooter back."

Alvaro sat down at the computer. "According to the notes, the passenger was abusive to the crew members who warned her. Sure you don't want to stick around? It's been a good six months or so since we have had to remove a passenger from the cruise and she bears all the hallmarks of the candidate to be the next one."

McKay covered his yawn with his hand. "I'll pass. I'm back on at noon. I need as much sleep as I can get."

He made it two steps out the door when Alvaro called him back in. "Mr. F is active on the camera."

This early in the morning? "I'll head over there now."

"Keep me updated over the comms."

McKay hurried through the crew prep areas to the eleventh deck. He stepped out into the hall.

Alvaro's voice came through the earpiece. "He is leaving."

McKay quickened his step, only to find the hallway empty. "Missed them."

"Better luck next time."

A door opened and Dana stepped into the hall dressed in leggings and a t-shirt.

"Good morning."

"Are you following me?"

"No, I was just checking on a problem."

"The banging on the wall?"

"You heard something?"

"More like someone who needed to find a room." Dana rolled her eyes. "Was that your problem?"

"Maybe. We are a family friendly cruise line." He tried to force a yawn down, but it escaped anyway.

"You look tired. Don't you ever sleep?"

"Usually. In fact, that was where I was headed." He needed to say something kind or witty, but his brain wouldn't work.

"Well then, I hope you sleep well. I'm off to do a quick workout."

"Walking all over Belfast won't be enough for you?" He hoped the question came out teasing.

"I need to strengthen my ankle. Stretches mostly."

"Have a good workout then." He paused at a crew access door, not caring which one it was. He was in danger of saying something stupid, like complaining about how good she looked in her work out leggings.

"Get some rest. I'll see you later."

McKay reached his room and his bed. As tired as he was, he should have fallen asleep instantly. Instead, his brain served up images of Dana. The move she used on that creep of a guy was more than impressive to him. He wondered if anyone not in security would find it as hot as he did. And the leggings... Sleep, he needed sleep. Time to start counting sheep like he'd told Gracie to do.

One day in Belfast wasn't enough. Dana would have preferred to explore the sites without everyone in the bridal party gawking like typical tourists. However, Cheyanne wanted photos in front of city hall. They hadn't planned on some sort of festival taking up most of the lawn space with food vendors. Chandler moved the photo opportunity to the steps of a cathedral. Then everyone returned to the city hall for lunch at the booths.

Left with a half day to explore, Dana made the best of it, choosing a tourist bus to give her the quick highlights. The guide, a retired teacher, had very strong political opinions about Belfast's difficult history. Although little remained of the bombings that had once torn the city apart, the guide's words brought much of the contention to life.

Too soon her phone alarm reminded her it was time to head back to the ship. She joined the long queue of passengers waiting to board. The woman ahead of her complained loudly to all who would listen about the cruise confiscating her scooter and then threatening to expel her from the ship. Dana opened her reading app and stared at it hoping to avoid conversation with the woman.

Concentrating on the words of the first chapter of her new book on the screen was useless. By the time she boarded the ship, Dana decided that the woman deserved to have her electric scooter impounded. Parking it in the hallway was a fire hazard.

The woman quieted as they neared the security check to scan their room cards. The rhythmic ping, ping was the loudest sound in the area.

Dana swiped her card.

"You!" Screeched the woman in front of her pointing at McKay. "You and your security men took my scooter away!"

"Ma'am, if you would please continue on." McKay gestured to the x-ray machine.

"I will not. I want to see you fired. Taking a way an old woman's scooter!"

Dana wondered why the woman had a scooter at all. She'd walked the length of the dock, if not more, since taxis weren't allowed beyond the port entrance.

The woman continued to hold up the line of passengers.

"Please, step aside. We have passengers trying to board." McKay's voice was calm and soothing.

A crew member in a security shirt and the chief security officer came down a side hallway.

The woman continued yelling. "I have my rights."

"Mrs. Rice, so nice to see you again. Will you please step aside?" Officer Alvaro's words were not a request.

One of the woman's friends prodded her. "Just drop it before they kick you off."

"No one is going to make me walk the plank. Do you know who I am?"

Dana bit her lip to keep from laughing.

"Mrs. Rice, you have two choices. Either move on or have us remove you from the ship."

The friend tugged at Mrs. Rice's arm. "Come on Jill. They are just doing their job."

"They wouldn't dare kick me off."

Not a wise move on the woman's part.

"Yes, they can. Look at his face Jill." The friend tugged harder, and the angry woman followed her to the X-ray machine.

Dana tried to catch McKay's eye, but he was focused on Officer Alvaro. One nice thing about working for Hastings is that her principals rarely yelled at her. And when they did, it was a child having a tantrum and she could pick him up and move him if necessary.

The crew member working the scanner stopped it and reversed the belt.

"Do you have a sandwich in your bag?"

"I didn't finish my lunch," responded Mrs. Rice.

"I'm afraid we need to dispose of it. It contains foods we can't bring aboard. Will you please open your bag?"

"I will not. I paid good money for that. I am not letting it go to waste."

Officer Alvaro moved to the scanner. "If you would like to finish it you may go back ashore and eat it."

"What is wrong with you people?" asked Mrs. Rice.

McKay switched places with the crew member who'd come with Officer Alvaro and joined the tech behind the scanner. McKay held out his hand to the security tech running the scanner so he could get the woman's bag.

"Don't you touch that, you thief."

"If you will please come with me." McKay pointed to the section of the gangway that allowed people to leave the ship.

Mrs. Rice looked from McKay to Officer Alvaro, weighing her options.

Was it terrible to wish for a full self-destruct? Dana wanted to see how McKay would handle things. So far, he'd kept a professional demeanor.

The woman harrumphed and walked over to the exit. McKay returned her bag to her. She paused and looked down the line of those trying to board. She fished a mustard stained napkin bulging with various meats from her bag and thrust it at McKay. "Forget it. Just throw this thing away."

He caught it too late and a blotch of yellow appeared on his pristine white uniform shirt. "If you will, please put your bag back on the scanner belt."

The woman thumped it down. And marched on through.

Dana passed closer to McKay. Their eyes met briefly, and she felt a spark of something—admiration, attraction, or something more complex. "Well done."

"Thank you."

Dana returned to her room, determined to finish the book she'd started. She went out to the balcony catching the last of the evening sun. The book had to wait for the sunset, it was too glorious to miss. Her fingers traced the railing to the cadence of the waves. The cooling evening air carried a hint of salt and possibility. As the last rays bounced across the waves, the cooling wind, chased her back into her room. She checked the time. McKay got off around ten, didn't he? What were the chances of running into him if she went top side?

There had to be more to what happened with Mrs. Rice. It was a flimsy excuse, and Dana knew it. She didn't care about the details—she just wanted to talk to him.

Mrs. Rice was an excuse. But sometimes, the best conversations start with the flimsiest of pretexts. She left her room hoping to find the best-looking security officer on the ship.

"Goodnight!" Gracie waved and blew kisses at the screen, ending the evening call. McKay slid his phone into his pocket and leaned against the railing. Needing a moment to transition back to work brain.

He'd kept the call short since he was still on duty. Six and a half days and he'd be home. Perhaps then he could help remove the tired look from his sister's face. He sighed and turned, intent on checking the aft bar before heading to the office.

Professional.

Focused.

His resolve wavered the moment he registered Dana walking toward him. Before his mind could catch up, a smile had already formed on his lips. "Good evening, Miss Knight."

She stopped a few feet from him, hugging her cardigan to her. "Still on duty, I see?"

The simple gesture sent an unexpected spark of awareness through him. McKay locked his professional demeanor firmly in place.

"Until midnight."

"Long day?"

"Odd day. I had shore leave yesterday that played a brutal game of musical schedules." If only he could tell her more. However, Alvaro commanded him not to recruit Dana. Any details he could share would be a dangerous step in that direction. She was too smart not to put it together.

"Coming up in the elevator, I heard that they kicked a woman off the ship today."

"Kicked off isn't the term we use, but yes, a passenger had to be removed from the cruise today."

"The woman in front of me when we returned to the ship?"

He waited for a moment to answer because he didn't want to be too obvious about how aware he'd been of her presence earlier. "That's right, you were there. She ruined my opportunity to say hello."

"I assume you can't tell me any details." She leaned back against the railing and looked up at him.

"Since you were there, I can tell you that she received multiple warnings and is fortunate to be disembarked in a city with an airport." He paused, not sure what to say next. "There is so much more to that story I can't tell."

Dana studied his face. "Don't worry, I won't pester you for details."

McKay laughed. "How about word to the wise, demanding to see the captain rarely works out well."

"She didn't!"

"I couldn't say."

Dana laughed. "I'll assume she did. That strategy never works on internet videos."

"Honestly, I don't think I've ever seen it work out for anyone."

Dana picked at the sleeve of her sweater. "If you are still working, I should probably move along."

"It was nice talking to you. See you later?"

"Maybe. Tomorrow we are staying the night in Dublin since the on board is so early and Cheyanne's bridesmaids have convinced her that she needs to do a pub crawl."

"You don't sound overly excited."

"I don't drink. I'm mostly going to make sure Cheyanne doesn't get talked into something she'll regret later."

"You're the designated driver?"

"One way to put it. Better than a babysitter."

McKay's phone vibrated. He looked down to see a message from Alvaro. "I need to go. Have a good evening."

"You too."

McKay hurried to the nearest crew door and entered before reading the message.

ALVARO: Activity on camera. Do walk by.

MAC: Going now.

He raced down the stairs as he reached the bottom of the last flight and his phone buzzed.

ALVARO: They moved on.

To avoid the stares of fellow crew members, McKay descended one more deck at a more sedate pace before crossing over to the crew elevator and retiring to the security office. Even if he had caught people kissing in that corner, the only thing he could do is leave the couple embarrassed. Likely, all it would have done was chase them into a new hiding spot. He doubted that either of the couple were stupid enough to do more than kiss, which wasn't against any cruise ship rules. There had to be another way to find the crew member that informed the fiancé about this spot. One that didn't involve Dana. She didn't deserve to be in the middle of this.

Twelve

THE SHELVES IN TRINITY LIBRARY towered over Dana, stretching into the grand ceiling above. Sunlight filtered through the tall windows, casting a warm glow on the rows of ancient tomes. Each shelf held row upon row of ancient books, their spines worn and faded with age. She walked slowly, taking in as much as she could without stalling the other tourists.

Visiting the library had been on her bucket list for years. The Book of Kells was interesting, but she'd rushed through the last few sections of the audio tour to get to this room filled with knowledge. She snapped a selfie to send to her dad, Brit, and Simone. Had McKay visited this room? What had he thought?

Dana stepped out of the way of a mom pushing a stroller. Where did thoughts about McKay come from? He wasn't here, and she was unlikely to be able to talk with him long enough to ask a question as trivial as his thoughts on Trinity Library. Yet he was the person she wanted to talk to about the day. The rest of the bridal party wouldn't care. Normally Cheyanne would, but with only days to the wedding, her time and thoughts were occupied.

When they'd made their excursion plans months ago, Dana was the only one who had wanted to visit the university, so they decided to spend the morning exploring and meet up at the hotel at check in time. Most of the party had opted for a tour of the world-famous brewery and a bus tour of the city, leaving her to enjoy the day alone.

As she left Trinity College and made her way down the cobbled sidewalk, Dana wished she could explore Dublin longer. She stopped at a small café for a quick lunch and continued her stroll through the city. Dana couldn't resist popping into a few shops along the way, searching for a sweater for her dad. The thought that the next store would have the perfect one and the fact she could return tomorrow kept her from purchasing the grey one she fell half in love with. It would look great on Dad, or McKay. No, the green one for McKay. One store later, the "what if she didn't make it back" thought won, and she retraced her steps for the sweater for her father.

She wished she could find something more for Dad. After a week dodging Sheila, Dana wondered if there was a way to show more appreciation for the man who gave up his military career to raise her. Nothing she saw on her way to rendezvous with Cheyanne gave her any ideas.

The hotel lobby buzzed with activity as Dana made her way inside. She spotted the rest of the bridal party gathered in a corner, chatting and laughing. Dana wound her way around tourists with roller bags and bell boys with carts.

Cheyanne handed Dana a room key. "Did you have a good time at Trinity?"

"The library was incredible. I wish I could have read one book, just to say I did." Reading a few paragraphs from the current novel on her phone wasn't the same thing.

"That's awesome," Cheyanne said. "We decided we're going shopping for matching tacky tourist shirts for the bachelorette party tonight."

Dana raised an eyebrow. "There is a chain store with plenty of those."

As they made their way to the shops, they chatted about the wedding. Amy-Kate seemed to be a bit tipsy. From the other bridesmaid's comments, she finished everyone's sample drinks on the brewery tour.

As they walked down the street, Amy-Kate tripped and fell on the cobblestone. She winced in pain as she tried to stand up. "I think I twisted my ankle," she slurred.

Dana helped her sit up against a nearby wall while Renee called for a taxi to take them back to the hotel.

"I'm sorry," Amy-Kate mumbled, tears in her eyes.

"It's okay," Dana reassured her. "Accidents happen. Do we need to go to a hospital?"

"No. I can just go back to the ship. If it gets worse, I'll see the doctor on board. My travel insurance will cover it." Amy-Kate rubbed her ankle. "Can I borrow your crutches? I'll be fine in a day or two."

"We could just stay in the hotel bar. Then you won't need to go back," suggested Lindie.

"If we wanted to stay in one place, we could all go back to the ship. They might refund our fees since we didn't really use the rooms," said Erin.

Chey bit her lip. "I don't think they'll do that. Our stuff is in our rooms."

"Don't cancel your night. Dublin pubs. You can't miss them." Amy-Kate used the wall to stand, putting no weight on her injury.

Renee offered a hand. "But you shouldn't go alone."

Dana looked at the time on her phone. "There is just enough time, I can take Amy-Kate back to the ship and meet up with you for dinner."

"Mom and Daddy will be on the ship tonight, so she won't be alone..." Chey's face was a mix of emotions.

"I can go myself," said Amy-Kate.

"Not through the train station. Remember how many stairs?" Lindie crossed her arms.

Cheyanne looked to Dana. "You don't mind?"

"Not as long as you get me one of the Celtic design shirts." Dana gave one of the practiced reassuring smiles she used with her principals when Alan Hastings was shouting in the coms device in her ear about a treat and she didn't want the principal to know.

The taxi pulled up. Dana helped Amy-Kate in and directed the driver to the nearest train station.

At the station, they called for the lift to take them down to the platform. A woman's voice came over the speaker, asking why they needed the lift. Dana quickly explained, and the door opened.

The digital sign indicated they had only four minutes for the next train's arrival for the short trip to the outer harbor where the cruise ship docked.

"Dana!"

Her heart leaped at the voice. She turned to see McKay weaving through the crowd in their direction. As he neared, she saw he had several bags in his hands.

"More souvenirs? I thought you said you had enough."

"Well..." He shifted his weight from foot to foot, moving the bags to one arm. "I am going to win the best uncle award."

He smiled brightly and Dana's heart did a little leprechaun leap of joy. His expression changed.

"I thought you weren't coming back to the ship."

"Amy-Kate twisted her ankle. I'm just escorting her back, getting her my crutches..."

The train arrived, ending the conversation. Dana wrapped her arm around Amy-Kate, acting as a human crutch. McKay did the same from the other side, his arm brushing Dana's, nearly causing her to forget the woman between them.

On board they found a double set of facing seats separated by a table. Amy-Kate sat on one side, her foot up on the bench seat. Dana took the window seat and McKay sat next to her. Amy-Kate looked from Dana to McKay and back, a smile crossed her lips.

Dana's mind raced. Amy-Kate was the type of woman who would use the information that there was a friendship between Dana and McKay to her advantage. Although she wanted a deep conversation with him, she knew she had already said too much. The fact he'd called her by her first name was a big give away. "Amy-Kate, have you met Mr. Worth? He is a security officer. He had to do a background check on me when we boarded. He was also at the dinner I ate with the captain."

Amy-Kate's eyes inspected McKay as if she were deciding which chocolate to purchase in a candy store. She turned back to Dana and her eyebrows rose. "You sound rather defensive to me."

Dana couldn't win, so she changed the subject. "Officer Worth, have you ever seen the Book of Kells?"

"Yes, I loved it." McKay gestured animatedly as he described the intricate designs and vibrant colors of the Book of Kells. He wasn't speaking in his normal manner. It took Dana a moment to realize he was actually quoting some of the dialogue from the audio tour. Turning the conversation into a monologue.

Amy-Kate rolled her eyes and looked at her foot and moaned.

Dana hid a smile. Her heart warmed at McKay's obvious attempt to deflect Amy-Kate's attention from their budding friendship. McKay had understood the assignment perfectly. Amy-Kate would have no reason to think there was an interest there. However, it raised more questions in Dana's mind. Questions she wanted to be alone to ask him. Just how much did they have in common?

McKay finished his duties, checking and rechecking the passenger count. The two-day stay in Dublin meant many passengers stayed in the city. A few had failed to tell the cruise line their plans, delaying closure of the ship for the night. With fewer passengers on board, McKay took advantage of his officer status to eat in the French-themed restaurant. As he made his way up to dinner, he noticed Dana sitting at a corner table of the promenade deck, gazing out into the vast ocean.

He blinked to be sure before approaching her. "Dana?"

She turned to him, her green eyes glistening with unshed tears. "Hi."

"How did you miss going back to shore?"

"Long story. I just finished calling Chey to tell her." She smiled wryly. "Guess I literally missed the boat on this one. At least we're close enough to shore that I could use my regular phone. Otherwise, I might have broken my promise about using the Hastings app."

"Then I would have been looking for you." He tried to make his voice light, but felt he failed. "I'm on my way to dinner. Want to join me?"

Oh, he shouldn't have asked that. Still, he wanted her to agree.

She thought for a moment, then shook her head. "Better not. Amy-Kate is suspicious, and she is the person who will pound on the door to the bridge until the Captain himself answers. I don't want to give anyone else reason to think that there's something going on—" Dana ended the thought with a little shrug.

"I'll be off at 2230, I mean 10:30."

"We use military time at work. No need to translate."

"We can meet here and talk." At that time of night, there was very little chance of a passenger coming near the closed buffet, and even if they did, the conversation was in a public place on opposite sides of the table. And in full view of not one, but two cameras. He would have to keep the conversation brief.

"I'd like that."

McKay nodded and headed off, entering a service area and then the restaurant. He spotted Dana's mother and stepfather across the room. Dana was wise not to come with him. Amy-Kate might have knocked on the bridge door, but from what he knew of Dana's mom, she would have pounded on the door to the captain's private quarters.

He finished his dinner alone, absentmindedly scrolling through his phone as he ate. He studied the video clip the hidden camera took the night before. Although the woman's face was hidden, McKay felt as if he'd seen her recently. The train earlier. Amy-Kate was the woman with Chandler Fairfax. He checked the other clips. How had he not seen the similarities before?

Thoughts of whether he should tell Dana about what he knew about her sister's fiancé raced through his mind. If Cheyanne was his sister, he would want her to know. If only someone had warned his sister Jen about the mistake she was making.

As he made his way through the ship, he bumped into Alvaro.

"Hey, Mac. Off shift?"

"Just finished."

"Anything noteworthy?"

McKay hesitated before responding. "I know who the woman is."

"Who? How?"

"On my train ride back, I met her. Amy-Kate. She is one of the bridesmaids."

Alvaro let out a low whistle. "Thanks for letting me know. I'll keep an eye on that situation."

"I doubt anything will happen on the camera tonight. Amy-Kate hurt her ankle, so she won't be walking around. The rest of the bridal party, minus Dana—who escorted her back—stayed in Dublin for the night. Which, FYI, I am going to go talk to Dana right now."

Alvaro pinched his lips together. "I know you want to say something to her about the affair. Wait until the last night. We need to know which crew member is telling passengers about the blind spots. More than one person's safety could depend on it."

"If it isn't discovered by the last night, I need to let her know. I wouldn't feel right not telling."

"Understood."

McKay nodded before continuing on his way to meet with Dana as planned.

He arrived at their designated meeting spot on the promenade deck and found Dana already there, sitting at one of the tables overlooking the ocean.

"Hey," she greeted him with a small smile.

"Hi." He took a seat across from her and leaned back in his chair. A message popped up on his phone.

> JEN: Gracie spending the night at Grandma's. No need for a call. Talk tomorrow.

"Do you need to go?" Dana pointed to his phone.

"No. Just my sister telling me to skip my nightly call to my niece."

"You call every night?"

"Depends on the cruise. European cruises the time difference makes my late night call the right time for bed. Caribbean cruses not so much. My sister uses me for a go to bed bribe. If I can't because of work, I message her early enough. So, what is your long story?"

"Not that long, really. I asked my mom if she'd check in on Amy-Kate and of course Shelia said no. I don't think she realizes forcing me to stay onboard to care for her also punishes Cheyanne."

"I'm sorry you couldn't go. On the bright side, no hangover tomorrow."

"I don't drink. But I wanted to be with my sister and make sure nothing goes wrong. In a group, they aren't likely to be targeted, but..."

"You've seen things?"

"Pretty much."

"Then you don't drink so you can be her bodyguard?"

"If only it were that easy." Dana's laugh carried a dark tone. "I can't drink even if I wanted to. I learned in college, to my embarrassment, the second alcohol hits my tongue, my gag reflex takes over. My dad thinks it is psychosomatic."

McKay searched for a definition of the word and hoped his face didn't betray his lack of vocabulary.

"When I was about three my Dad was deployed. Mom threw a party. Next morning I woke up, and she was still asleep. I was thirsty and found what I thought was fruit punch like they had at daycare. It wasn't. I threw up everywhere. Mom and her friend, the 'daddy' I didn't like, were so mad at me."

"It wasn't your fault."

"Nope. Every time I smelled drinks after that, I lost my lunch, dinner, or whatever. I was about ten when Dad put it all together. It played a role in him finally getting full custody of me. I grew out of the smelling it and reacting phase, but last time I checked, I still can't drink. Which isn't a bad thing."

"I agree to that. I don't drink onboard because I always want to be alert. On my months off, I may drink a toast at a wedding or something, but not much more."

"Good to know."

"What are your plans for tomorrow?"

"Find Cheyanne. And have a low-key day sightseeing. Late lunch with her fiancé and likely, her parents."

McKay's phone vibrated.

ALVARO: Watching them come from different directions toward the meeting spot. Go down. Send your friend to her room first.

They must have located him talking to Dana on CCTV.

McKAY: On my way.

ALVARO: Her first.

Orders were orders. "I need to go. May I escort you down?"

Dana hesitated for a moment before answering, "Sure. That sounds nice." She stood up and grabbed her phone.

They walked together in comfortable silence to the elevator, only passing one person. When the elevator doors opened, McKay placed his hand in the center of Dana's back to guide her in. She blushed. He dropped his hand. She stepped away.

McKay took a step back. "Sorry. I shouldn't—"

Dana eyed the mirrored elevator ceiling. "The camera is hidden well."

The doors slid open at her deck and they stepped off. Dana held up her hand. "This is as far as you go. I don't want you getting into trouble for fraternizing with passengers."

"I wish I could."

Her eyes widened. She turned and walked a couple of steps before looking back. "Goodnight McKay. I wish you could too."

She turned into the corridor, leaving McKay momentarily rooted to the spot. Remembering his duty, he turned into the opposite corridor and entered the crew door. He hoped this worked—he couldn't send Dana to do this again.

Thirteen

Why? Why? Why? Had Cupid failed archery? Was she born under some morose cloud? Every time she found a man she wanted to be with, some obstacle stood in their way. For a moment when he touched her back, she wanted to melt into him, experience the hug she craved. Her heart didn't understand what her mind had been telling it for the past two days—McKay was off limits. Why had his hand lingered in that forbidden touch? Could he be struggling as much as she was?

A sound ahead made her look up from the floor. A woman with red hair walked quickly down the corridor. Amy-Kate? It couldn't be. She needed crutches, and why would she be down on this deck? Full of curiosity, Dana walked faster.

The woman passed Dana's room and turned a corner, allowing Dana a glimpse of her profile. It was Amy-Kate. Dana slowed her steps as she reached her room. Should she follow Chey's friend?

Voices reached her—a man and woman talking in hushed tones—and then she heard her own name. She stuffed her room key back in her pocket and moved closer to the corner.

"I told you, Dana won't be a problem. She's down on Deck 8 or somewhere in one of those inner rooms. She won't find us, and no one else is in our suite. Can't we just go there?"

"Baby, we can't risk being seen." The man spoke with a British accent.

"But I'm tired of hiding in this corner even if no cameras can see us," Amy-Kate's sentence ended with a deep throaty moan. "Stop, that, I'm, trying, to—"

"We can converse in public." It almost sounded like Cheyanne's fiancé.

"I've orchestrated this event so we could be alone. There's no one else in our suite. We can just go up there. Dana and her mom—"

Dana's stomach churned as the pieces clicked into place. She turned the corner.

The couple leaned in the corner with Amy-Kate pinned against the wall. Chandler's head buried in Amy-Kate's neck. His hands. Well, his hands shouldn't have been touching Cheyanne's friend anywhere. Amy-Kate noticed first. She pushed Chandler away.

It took a moment for Dana to find words. "Wow, your ankle healed quickly. And Chandler, fancy running into you here."

Chandler turned. His face red with anger. He glared at Dana. "Where did you come from?"

"That isn't the question, is it? Why is my sister's fiancé making out with her good friend and bridesmaid in a corridor?"

He stepped menacingly toward her. "You are going to forget what you saw."

"And let my sister marry you without all the facts? I don't think so."

"Keep! Quiet!" Chandler punctuated each word with a pointed finger.

Dana's training kicked in automatically as she assessed his body language—he was building toward violence. She stepped back to give herself more room in case he attacked. "How long has this been going on?"

Amy-Kate tugged on Chandler's arm. He shrugged her off and lunged at Dana.

Dana turned and caught his wrist at the same time. Using his momentum, she pinned him face first against the wall. "How long have you been cheating on my sister?"

As he struggled against her grasp, he cursed in British and American English, showcasing a rather limited and unimaginative vocabulary.

Running footfalls came from both directions.

"Let him go." McKay didn't use her name. Dana dropped her hold and stepped back.

Officer Alvaro came from the opposite direction. A female security officer stood behind him. "What is going on here?"

Amy-Kate and Chandler started yelling at once. Dana waited for someone to stop them.

"We are disturbing passengers. Let's take this into the security office," said Officer Alvaro.

"Fine, then you can expel this woman from the ship. I'd like to press assault charges." Chandler pointed at Dana.

Dana fought to keep her expression neutral, though inside she was seething. She assumed there would be video footage of him lunging at her. Technically, she'd acted in self-defense. Although there had been a good dose of anger mixed in, and she used more force than was strictly necessary.

Not surprisingly, once they reached the security offices, the officers separated the three of them. The chief security officer took Chandler into his office, McKay led Amy-Kate into a conference room, and the female officer sat with Dana at a corner table.

"Miss Dana Knight, correct?" The officer opened her tablet.

"Yes."

"I'm Martina. I'll save you some time. The video caught him jumping, no there is a better English word…" The officer's face scrunched up. "Lunging. That's the word for it. He was lunging at you. I am surprised you to—" She paused for a moment before saying, "You know what I mean. Sorry, I was just speaking Tagalog with my friends in the crew lounge and my brain isn't back in English mode."

"Pinned him to the wall?"

"Yes. I have not seen many women do something like that unless they were a superhero in a movie. You work for a security company, right?"

"Yes, I do."

"Is that where you learned to defend yourself like that?"

"Yes. The original owner's wife and her daughter are passionate about women defending themselves. They've developed several techniques to help women use their natural structure to their advantage."

Martina leaned forward, clearly intrigued. "That sounds fascinating. I need a course like that. Even though we have some CCTV footage, I am supposed to ask you what happened."

It wasn't a question, but Dana answered anyway. "I was returning to my cabin and saw Amy-Kate. Which struck me as odd as she twisted her ankle earlier today. She turned the corner just beyond my new cabin. I wasn't going to keep following her, but then I heard her say my name. As soon as I realized she was talking to my sister's fiancé..." Dana censored out her emotions. "I confronted them." Saying her reasons out loud, Dana wondered if she was justified in her actions. "Chandler lunged at me with a raised fist, and I defended myself."

"Understandable—if I caught my sister's fiancé cheating, I'd be upset, too." Martina looked down at her tablet. "That seems to be all I have to ask you. You are free to go. You know your way out of here?"

"Yes." Dana glanced at the two closed doors. It's odd that Martina didn't ask her more questions. Wasn't she the one in trouble? Chandler didn't actually hit her, he just tried. Why would McKay need to talk to Amy-Kate longer than Martina interrogated her? Not that it was much of an integration. It barely qualified for taking a statement. Not a single follow-up question. They must rely heavily on the CCTV. Amy-Kate hadn't been aggressive.

McKay responding as quickly as he had made sense. He'd barely left her. But the Chief Security Officer Alvaro and Martina, who was a single bar officer, also being that close? Odd coincidence or something else?

A wave of exhaustion hit her as the adrenaline wore off. She had bigger concerns now. What would she tell Cheyanne?

McKay handed Amy-Kate another tissue and tried to mask his disgust. "Do you know who told Chandler about the meeting place?"

Through her tears, Amy-Kate sniffled, wiping her eyes. "I—I don't know."

"It's okay, take your time." It had taken long enough to get Amy-Kate to divulge that the meeting place was chosen because Chandler knew there were not security cameras there.

"He told me he paid handsomely for it... I'd complained because I felt cheap sneak—sneak—sneaking around." She wailed and burst into sobs.

McKay pushed the tissue box in front of her. He'd seen better acting in first day rehearsals.

Between shuddering breaths, Amy-Kate managed to speak. "Dana's going to tell Chey and ruin everything."

Maybe she knew more. "Ruin what?"

"He was getting me an apartment in London. Now the wedding will be off, and Chandler's father will—"

There were no words. McKay hoped his face remained neutral. Was he hearing correctly? Cheyanne's fiancé was setting up Amy-Kate to be his mistress, and she was fine with the plan. He couldn't ask. It had nothing to do with ship security. "Do you know when Chandler paid this person?"

She stopped her fake sobs and looked at him, eyes narrowing. "What does that have to do with anything?"

"As ship's security, we don't care what you are doing in your private life as long as it is consensual. However, I am very concerned that someone is selling the location of our CCTV blind spots to Chandler and perhaps others."

"Oh." Amy-Kate looked down at her hands. "I don't know when he arranged it for sure, but he texted me the day before we flew to London that he had found a place for us to meet. I thought he purchased another room."

"When did he tell you the location?"

"The first night we were on board, he showed me the place. Very disappointing if you ask me. He said he didn't want the temptation of a suite."

Not very helpful information, even if it did explain why someone as well off as Chandler would pay someone for just a corner. Apparently, the man had a modicum of honor and didn't get a room for his mistress the week before the wedding. "Thank you for your help, Amy-Kate. You may return to your suite."

An odd look came over Amy-Kate's face. "Chey is going to kick me out. Where will I go? Are there any more rooms on the ship?"

"Sorry, not my department. You can see guest services in the morning." If she was wise she'd disembark and head to the Dublin Airport.

Amy-Kate stood, talking more to herself than McKay. "Maybe Dana would trade, no I don't want a dungeon room."

Interesting. Dana hadn't told the others, or at least Amy-Kate, about her new room. Still not his problem. He watched until Amy-Kate turned the corner and out of sight. Alvaro's office door was still closed. Hopefully, Alvaro got the answers he needed. McKay watched the monitors on the walls. A few people still tried their luck in the casino. The bars were mostly empty.

"Anything of interest?" he asked the single security officer watching the monitors.

"No, Sir." The new security employee still used the honorific term.

The empty chair in front of the other monitors caught McKay's attention. "Has Ian been gone long?"

"He said he needed to take a break just after you all came in."

McKay checked his watch. Just shy of a half hour. Long for an unscheduled break. Two crew members hurried into the office. One was still tucking his shirt in. "Reporting, Sir."

Before McKay could ask what they were reporting for Alvaro opened his door. He looked first at McKay, then the empty seat in front of the monitors. The frown on the chief security officer's face deepened. "Change of plan, you two go find Ian and bring him here. He may resist. Mac escort Mr. Fairfax to his cabin. He will be packing, as he has chosen to disembark in the morning. I'll send someone to replace you as soon as I am able to and then we can talk."

Chandler held his head high as he left the room. McKay wondered why he was leaving. Was it to avoid charges? Or his bride-to-be and her family?

Once they were in the elevator, Chandler spoke. "I reported your assignations with Cheyanne's sister. Expect your comeuppance too."

McKay ignored him. Once they reached the cabin, McKay stood outside the door. He only had to wait a few minutes for two security crew members to relieve him. They would stay at their posts until Chandler left the ship.

In the brief silence of the corridor, McKay's thoughts drifted to Dana. She needed an explanation. He pushed them aside—he had a job to finish.

The captain stood in Alvaro's office. "Any idea how long this has been going on?"

"Ian isn't talking. The dark web chat post that Mr. Fairfax responded to was two months old. I have to wonder if Ian's done this before." Alvaro shook his head. He turned to McKay. "Did the redhead know anything?"

"Only that Mr. Fairfax paid for the information about the space. She seemed more upset about her future than anything."

The captain stared up at the ceiling. "This could have been so much worse. I can't say I liked your sting operation, but I am glad it worked. Good idea, Worth."

The implications hung heavy in the room—a security breach like this could have devastating consequences. Neither Alvaro or McKay put words to what the captain was thinking. It wasn't necessary.

"It was Martina's plan. She deserves the credit." McKay pondered his interactions with the soon to be ex-crew member. "You know Ian doesn't strike me as being bright enough to come up with this on his own."

"I had the same thought," agreed Alvaro. "I'm glad we kept the operation only to the three of us. We might have missed Ian entirely."

The captain stifled a yawn. "I'll contact the main office and let them know our suspicions. They will need to consult with legal to see if there are any laws that have been broken. Between the laws of the US, UK, and the Netherlands, there must be something. I don't want to be forced to turn Ian loose so he can try this on another cruise line."

Netherlands? Could the country their ship sailed under do anything? Ninety percent of cruise ships sailed under convenience flags. Meaning they claimed one home country, even though mainly operating out of another. The home country rarely came into play except in docking priority. McKay fought the urge to yawn, too. "Don't forget Ireland, we discover the issue in their waters."

The captain shook his head. "So glad I won't have to figure out this mess. It's a shame we had an innocent bystander in this. I watched the footage. I'm impressed with how quickly she stopped Mr. Fairfax when he became aggressive. Wasn't she the one on crutches at dinner?"

"Yes, sir," answered Alvaro. "She works for Hastings Security."

The captain closed his eyes for a moment. "Please tell me she isn't onboard working."

"I've spoken to her on several occasions, and I am convinced that Miss Knight is here only as the sister of the bride," said McKay.

"Hastings Security, what are the chances of that? Did she know what was going on?" asked the captain.

"Miss Knight had no idea about the hidden camera or the rendezvous spot." The fact sat like an anchor in McKay's stomach.

"Well, if it is appropriate, thank her. And if Mr. Fairfax tries to charge her with anything, let her know I am all for testifying against him." The captain seemed to have aged in the past few moments. If Ian wasn't working alone the ramifications were enormous.

McKay nodded his reply. He had no intention of telling Dana anything unless it came up. If he did, it wouldn't take long for her to realize that she'd been manipulated into an awkward position and could ruin any connection they had forged. But keeping the truth from her felt just as wrong as using her had been. Either way, he'd never have a chance to know her better.

Fourteen

THERE ARE A FEW THINGS less pleasant to wake up to than somebody pounding on your door. Dana threw off her covers and padded over to the door. Through the peephole she saw her mother's fist raised, ready to pound again.

"Just a minute!" Dana ran her fingers through her hair and glanced in the mirror, glad she took the time to make sure all the mascara was off last night.

Sheila pounded again as Dana opened the door.

"It's about time!" Her mother pushed her way into the room.

Dana counted to ten as her dad had taught her, and bit her lip to keep in any comment she might have felt compelled to utter. Such as the fact it was before sunrise. Taking a deep breath, she waved her mother over to the couch. "Good morning to you too, mother."

"Don't you sass me. I've been up all night with Amy-Kate, who's crying her eyes out. We decided that you should trade rooms with her, and I went down to your room and you weren't there!"

Dana sat on her bed and tried to respond as calmly as possible. "No, I was here."

"How did you get this room?"

"There was a problem with my old room."

"Well, this room will be better for Amy-Kate."

"I am not switching rooms again."

"Oh yes, you will. I paid for that room you had."

"And I paid for my space in Cheyanne's suite, which was more than the value of that interior room you stuffed me into. I have more than paid for my reservations." Dana tried to push her anger down, but she hadn't had enough sleep to do it successfully.

"Well, now you can be in Cheyanne's suite with her."

"I don't want to change rooms again. I am quite fond of this one."

"Amy-Kate can't stay there."

"She isn't my problem." The repercussions of her actions may be, but Amy-Kate made choices that came with consequences.

"Well, you're the one who ruined everything!"

"If you wouldn't mind keeping your voice down. I'm sure my neighbors do not appreciate being woken by your yelling."

Sheila lowered her voice a decibel or two. "I am not yelling. I am trying to save a marriage. To do that, I need you to change rooms with Amy-Kate."

"Save a marriage? You want your daughter to marry a man you know is being unfaithful?"

"Mitchell needs the business connections."

The words hit Dana as if her mother had slapped her. A thought almost too terrible to say out loud formed in Dana's mind. "Did you know about Chandler's affair?"

Sheila turned her face to the window where the first gray mists of day dotted the seascape.

"You did." Dana drew in a breath. "That is why you moved me from the Diamond Suite and put me in economy. You knew I would figure it out."

"You've always been too observant." Sheila sniffed. A familiar gesture—prelude to tears that never quite materialized. Next, she would ask for a tissue.

How could she have knowingly let Chey marry a man who wasn't worthy of her? Anger worse than what Dana faced in her youth boiled up. Sheila needed to leave now, or security might have a reason to detain Dana.

"I am not changing rooms." Dana stood. "Now please excuse me. I am going to get ready for the day."

"You just can't dismiss me. I am your mother."

Any shred of patience Dana held on to evaporated. "Only when it seems to be convenient for you."

Her mother gasped. "What a terrible thing to say."

"I don't want to fight with you. Not now. I need to get ready so I can go as soon as possible."

"You are not to tell your sister."

"What I say to my sister is not for you to dictate."

"But you'll ruin the wedding."

"Amy-Kate and Chandler did that. Not me."

"But the wedding—England. We've spent so much money. The connections." The last words revealed her mother's only real concern. Money.

"Then I suggest you go pound on Chandler's door. Since he's the one who ruined everything, he can pay for it."

"But if she forgives him, everything will work out."

Don't say it. DON'T say it. Dana said it anyway. "I'm sure my father has a different opinion about a cheating spouse and things working out."

Sheila raised her hand to slap Dana's face.

Dana easily sidestepped. "Please leave or I will call security."

"Fine, I'll leave, but don't you dare tell your sister anything."

Dana wasn't about to make that promise. Chey needed to know.

Sheila slammed the door on her way out. Dana sent a whispered apology into the cosmos for the passengers her mother disturbed.

Foregoing breakfast, Dana was one of the first in the queue to leave the ship. Chandler, accompanied by Officer Alvaro and another security member, was at the front of the line with two large suitcases. Apparently, he was going to take the coward's way out and sneak off the ship before Cheyanne could return. Dana studied the group. From the stern look on the chief security officer's face, there might be more to that story. What exactly had Chandler done?

She wasn't close enough to hear any conversation between Chandler and his somewhat disheveled best man. Their clipped responses to each other indicated an argument. Unfortunately, she couldn't read lips, though she was fairly certain she heard Cheyanne mentioned repeatedly. Had Chandler contacted her sister yet?

The men left the ship together. Dana waited for her turn to disembark. By the time she reached the port gates, neither man was around. Nor were they at the train station. Dana spent most of the twenty-minute ride thinking of things to say to her sister. Oh, to be three again and not understand the blow she was delivering when uncovering infidelity. Judging from her conversation with her mother and depending on who told Cheyanne about the affair, there were multiple ways this morning could go. There was the real possibility Dana would be the one to deliver the news.

Few people were on the streets as she walked to the lavish hotel. Dana found Cheyanne's room and knocked on the door.

Erin opened it and let her in. "Don't talk too loudly. We all have wicked hangovers."

Cheyanne stepped out of the bathroom, her hair wrapped in a towel. "I don't have a hangover. Every time someone offered to buy me a drink, I thought of your worried look. I stuck to soda all night long."

"What worried look?"

Cheyanne tipped her head. "The one you are using now. What is wrong? Is Amy-Kate's ankle broken?"

Dana's throat tightened. Her sister's concern for Amy-Kate made this even harder. "You haven't talked to her today?"

"No." Cheyanne sat on the end of a bed.

"What about Chandler?"

"No. We aren't meeting until noon."

Dana bit her lip. The scenario she most feared. She sat next to Cheyanne.

"What is it? You're scaring me."

"Perhaps we should talk in private."

Cheyanne shook her head. "It was Amy-Kate, wasn't it? She is the one Chandler has been cheating on me with."

That her sister already suspected unfaithfulness was not a possibility Dana had thought through. "You knew?"

"I suspected something. I just hoped—" Cheyanne leaned into Dana's side and cried. Lindie, Erin, and Renee slipped out of the room.

Dana wrapped her arm around her sister, wishing she could shield her from more than just this moment's pain. If Dana ever saw Chandler again, she would hit him. As for Sheila, Dana would carry her role in this to the grave, or at least for a few days. One blow was enough for the morning. There was a chance her mother would confess her role in the debacle herself. Not much, but a chance.

Only one port left. McKay rubbed the back of his neck, trying to loosen the knot that had been growing all day. Dana and her sister had returned to the ship earlier than most passengers. Shortly after, Amy-Kate had disembarked with more luggage than she could manage. The wedding was off. A sense of guilt gnawed at him.

McKay pushed the guilt aside the best he could. It wasn't his fault that Chandler was unfaithful. Yet he could have let it be known days ago. Would it have made a difference? He told himself likely not, but the rationalization felt hollow.

The wind whipped around the ship as they headed south. He completed a round of the empty upper decks hoping that Dana might be sitting in the alcove where they met before. A couple played a game of cards in the spot.

In the library, the sole occupant was a leprechaun rubber duck tucked into a cushion. He left it for a passenger to find. Since he didn't have to clean the ship, McKay found the tradition of passengers hiding ducks cute. Gracie would love to find one or two if she ever sailed. Crew members kept a bucket full of the most unique duckies they'd found in the crew lounge. Pink cowgirl, pirate, and zombie ducks all found their way to the bucket during the few hours when the crew cleaned the ship for the next cruise. They also displayed a board showing the funniest places duckies had been found. Most passengers hid them respectfully, avoiding bathrooms, the buffet, and crew areas. He should take one from the crew area to Gracie. There had to be room in his luggage somewhere.

Dana wasn't in any of the public areas. With a resigned sigh, McKay opened the communications app from Ogilvie Inc. Would it work? McKay typed in Dana Knight and his heart jumped when her name popped up.

> Mac: How did your day go?

There was a pause before a message appeared.

> Dana: Security told me not to use this app on board.

> Mac: I think you're ok.

> Dana: My day went as expected. No wedding.

> Mac: How is your sister?

> Dana: Better than expected. His parents are livid and are on her side, so that is helpful. Especially

since Chey shipped most of her belongings over to their home. Sheila is a mess. We are ignoring her.

Mac: And you?

He held his breath, waiting for her response.

Dana: Curious.

Mac: About what?

Dana: Why was Chandler escorted off the ship?

Mac: Not sure I can say. Legal is still dealing with things.

Dana: Okay.

Mac: Any plans for tomorrow?

Dana: I still want to *air* kiss the Blarney Stone. Trying to talk Chey into going. She says she wants alone time.

Mac: The castle and stone are worth it. The line can be a pain, but it is one of those things you should do once if you have the chance.

Dana: You've been?

Mac: Yes. When I was a teenager on a family vacation. For the record, it worked for my sister.

Dana: Chey says she doesn't need to because she already has more words than she can say to Chandler.

Mac: Tell her she can deliver the words more eloquently.

She was with her sister. No point in continuing to look for her.

Alone in his room. McKay made his nightly call to his sister. Gracie was yawning and went to bed without a fuss.

"Are you sad to leave the cruise? You look a bit down?" asked Jen.

He tried to school his features into something less miserable. "Not really. I mean, it is just work."

"Then what is it?"

"I forced a passenger into an awkward situation and now I am wondering if I should have handled things differently."

"Explain."

"I can't say much."

"Tell me what you can. It may help you work through things."

By the time McKay finished explaining what he could, he felt worse.

Jen pondered before answering. "Obviously, I don't get all the parts you omitted, but having the wedding called off was a good thing. Believe me, no one wants to marry a cheater. It would have been nice if it had been earlier in the cruise, but still awkward."

"True. It is more that I put her sister in that situation."

"Did you order the room change?"

"No."

"Then not your problem. If it really bothers you, tell the sister. Although I don't see a point. It isn't like you'll see her again."

"I want to." Admitting it made the possibility seem to evaporate like sea foam.

"What?"

"I want to figure out a way to see Dana again. Away from the ship."

"Where you can date?"

"Pretty much."

"Okay, that is unexpected." Jen's smile grew.

"I just think she'll think less of me." The thought of Dana despising him made his chest ache.

Jen toyed with a pen. "That is a possibility. But if there is an investigation, I don't see how you can say anything to her."

"I know, I don't like it, but I know."

"She is in security, she will understand… Maybe."

"I hope so." It was all he could do.

Fifteen

Kissing the blarney stone didn't solve anything other than giving Dana some good quality time with a bunch of strangers. She found a quiet area on the castle grounds and pulled out her phone to text her friends.

> DANA: The wedding is off.

BRIT: What?

SIMONE: What?

> DANA: I caught Chandler cheating with one of the bridesmaids. I feel terrible. Trying to decide if I should come home early or tour London.

BRIT: Tour London.

SIMONE: I can send you my Jane Austen ultimate tour. You can do it all from the train. Mostly. You'll have to take a taxi to Lyme Regis.

BRIT: Definitely go to Bath.

Simone: You better not come home early. Use your planned PTO.

Dana: How detailed is your itinerary?

Simone: Places to stay, eat, essential things to see based on how long you are in a town. Since I usually have 2 days to explore. It is all by train.

Dana: Send it. I don't know what I'll have time for. Or if I am expected anyplace. I don't want to leave Chey alone, but Renee is her Maid of Honor for good reason. She's fantastic.

It hurt that Chey's friends were a greater comfort, but Renee did know her sister better than she did.

Brit: Bath. Sally Lunn bun, clotted cream. All you need to know.

Simone: She has to go to Lyme too. After all the Cobb and Captain Wentworth.

Dana: You know the difference between fiction and reality, correct?

Simone: Haha. A girl can dream.

Brit: I thought you kind of met someone.

Dana: Kind of is as close as it gets for me.

Simone: You could see him after the cruise, right?

Dana: Only if we plan to. He is going home to Indiana.

BRIT: What a coincidence, you are moving there with the Ogilvies aren't you?

DANA: I'll still be over an hour away from him.

SIMONE: It would take some effort. Is he worth it?

Dana stared at her screen. Was McKay worth a two-hour drive? Maybe once. If it went poorly, she could return home and say it was too far next time. But if it went well. That would be a lot of driving, and what happened when he returned to the cruise line? She learned from dad, long-distance relationships brought problems.

DANA: Not sure. I don't see this going anywhere. Eventually he'll go back out to sea and as fun as cruises are, I don't think I could ever work on one. Not doing a long-distance relationship.

There was the family thing too. Someday she wanted to be a mother. The Ogilvie kids had shown her that, and a spouse who was gone nine months out of the year didn't work with those plans.

BRIT: You should at least go on an actual date. One where you could hold hands or whatever without cruise ship rules.

SIMONE: Three dates. One to impress, one that's a mess, and one to confess.

DANA: Never heard of that. What does it mean mess and confess?

BRIT: It rhymes. 3rd date is to decide for yourself how you feel. NOT confess your feelings to him.

SIMONE: And the second date almost always goes poorly. It is a thing. So messy.

> Dana: Hence the reason I never get to a third date. The second ones are messes.

Brit: Tian calls the second the false loss. If you stop there, you'll never know.

> Dana: I know after one.

Simone: Then one date.

> Dana: Fine. Next time I see him, I'll invite him on a date. Only I'll have to go to his place. He can't know about the Ogilvies until he has had a background check.

Brit: That works.

The alarm on Dana's phone vibrated, if she didn't hurry, she would miss her bus.

> Dana: I gotta go. TTFN.

The phone vibrated with goodbyes as she crossed the grounds to the tour bus. At the gate, she ran into the last person she wished to see today—her mother.

"What are you doing sightseeing when your sister is heartbroken?"

"Cheyanne said she didn't need me." The other bridesmaids were more than smothering her. "I came to kiss the Blarney Stone."

"You are so selfish." Her mother followed Dana to the bus. Dana quickened her pace. Her mother grabbed her wrist and spun her around. "Don't you walk away from me."

"I have nothing else to say on the matter."

"Of course not. You ruined another marriage, just like you ruined mine."

"I was three years old. Not even old enough to understand you were cheating. All I did was tell Dad he was my favorite father, that I didn't like the other one who came to the house when he was gone. How was I supposed to know you were having an affair and to keep it a secret?"

"You were told not to tell!"

Fellow passengers heading for the buses looked their way as they passed. Dana lowered her voice. "If you had been dating a nicer person, I might not have. I didn't like the man you were dating slapping me. I wanted to be with my dad. He never once hit or spanked me." Dana didn't add that her mother had more than once.

"Of all the impertinent children. How did I get saddled with you?"

The question had been asked enough times that it didn't hurt anymore. Across the parking lot, the bus honked. Dana wrenched her hand free and ran to the bus, knowing her mother needed to find whatever transportation she'd come in.

The tour bus doors closed behind Dana and she searched for an empty seat. A blue-haired woman in a bright fuchsia blouse moved her bag, a sign Dana could sit next to her. The woman pointed out the window to where Dana's mother stood staring at the bus, her hands on her hips. "Is that your mum?"

"Yes. Don't worry, she's not on this bus. She took a different tour."

"How odd that you would take a different tour than your mother."

"If you saw us fighting, it isn't nearly as odd as you say. To put it politely, we don't get on."

"How long has that been going on?" The woman's soft accent soothed Dana's nerves.

Not in a mood to sugarcoat things, Dana told the stranger the truth. "Since I was three. She had an affair. I accidentally spilled the beans to my dad. She's never forgiven me."

"That's a shame. Mothers and daughters shouldn't be like that."

"One would think, wouldn't they? Do you have a family?" Dana asked to change the subject.

"I have a daughter who lives in the states and a son in the Royal Navy."

"You must be proud. "

"Yes. But I get lonely. It would be nice to see them more often than I do. Even so, I have my fun."

"You're from England then?"

"I live in London. Every year for our anniversary, we take a trip. Sadly, these past two years I've gone without my dear husband."

"My condolences. Did you have fun on this cruise?"

"I met some wonderful people. And some are not so nice. Did you hear a young man jilted his bride-to-be on our cruise?"

"That was my sister. And why my mother was yelling at me."

"Oh my. I didn't mean to gossip. So, you are part of the big bridal group then? It must have been a lovely hen party until it ended."

"It was. We made lots of memories. My sister is more about making sure everyone had some fun than everything being about her."

"When was she to be wed?"

"This Friday."

"She may not think so, but it was fortunate that she found out before the vows were said."

"She knows."

"Forgive me for being a nosey old woman. I shouldn't have asked. I'm Hermione, by the way. Like the girl in that wizard book you kids all seemed to love. However, I am not magical."

"You raised my spirits. That's magic enough for me." Dana smiled to prove her point.

"What are you going to do now that there is no wedding?"

"I'm going to go out to Bath and see everything I can and probably head down to Lyme Regis."

"Ah, you're a *Persuasion* fan."

"Guilty as charged."

"Do you have a Captain Wentworth in your life?"

Dana's cheeks warmed.

Hermione chuckled.

"Not really. We're not in a position to start a relationship."

"If it's meant to be, it is meant to be."
Too bad it wasn't that easy.

The tech stopped the X-ray machine. Another bottle of whiskey. Why passengers thought that they could sneak liquor on board, McKay would never know. It was so much easier just to declare it and turn it over to the crew so it could be returned at disembarkment. He waved the passenger over to Martina, who was in charge of checking in the liquor.

McKay turned back to the queue of passengers. A few people away, Dana laughed with an older woman he'd seen several times during the cruise. The women scanned their ID Cards.

"Welcome back on board. Did you have a good day?"

The older woman answered first. "Indeed, I did. I didn't attempt to kiss the Blarney Stone. I don't need to seeing as I already have the gift of gab."

"And you?" McKay looked at Dana.

"Does air kissing count?"

"After 2020, I say it's the best way."

The older woman whispered conspiratorially, "Don't let her tell you it worked. She isn't talkative at all. However, I got her to blush when I asked her if she had a beau and she won't tell me who it is."

Dana's instant blush was impossible to miss. She turned away and sent her backpack through the machine.

"Aha, see, just like—" the woman looked from Dana to McKay. "In fact, sir, you're blushing a bit too."

Dana hurried on and the woman looked at them both again, a large smile grew on her face.

McKay nodded and greeted the next person. The last thing he needed was for a passenger to think that there was something going on and report it. Because of the removal of Ian from the ship, they were down two crew members as Alberto left the ship to accompany Ian back to headquarters, leaving McKay and the other junior officers with extra duties.

An hour later another officer relieved him and McKay went to the security office where all the paperwork that Alvaro usually filed waited for him. Paperwork was, of course, a misnomer, as everything was filed electronically. He signed and dated the last form. In less than 24 hours, he'd be on land again.

With the few hours he had remaining on board, he was unlikely to find more than a few minutes to say hello to Dana. He desperately wanted to discover the meaning behind that blush and gain her permission to contact her once they were both home. He stared at the computer. He could access her cell phone number. His fingers hovered for a moment over the keys before he pushed the thought aside. Not only was there an ethics question involved, but he preferred that women gave him their phone numbers willingly. The company would deactivate his ship app access during his leave, causing him to lose that contact.

Maybe if he were very lucky, he could find her one more time before they reached Southampton.

Dana spent most of the afternoon in her cabin trying to read between all of the visitors knocking on her door. Cheyanne came by to escape her former bridesmaids, who were smothering her with attention. Minutes after her arrival, Sheila knocked. Dana barely opened the door before Cheyanne was at her side.

"Mom. I told you I don't want to see you for the rest of the day. I'm trying to process that you knew about this and didn't tell me. Can you go find a very short plank, please?"

"A plank? You know I can't do that exercise."

Dana couldn't hold back the laugh, earning her a glare from her mother.

Sheila tried to push her way in.

Dana blocked the way.

Cheyanne ducked between Dana and the door. "I didn't say to go exercise. I told you to find a plank as in 'walk the plank.' I've asked you politely to leave me alone, and it hasn't worked. I am tired of being polite."

Their mother took a step back, and Dana closed the door. Immediately, her mother started pounding.

Dana nodded to the balcony. "We can go out there and ignore her."

"I should have stood up to her years ago. I don't think I ever would've gotten engaged to him if it hadn't been for her and Daddy. I didn't see they wanted the connection so much. Daddy isn't nearly as pushy as Mom." Cheyanne sat down. "Daddy was the one who introduced me. I think he believes he could expand his company to England with such connections. Although Chandler said he couldn't. Daddy knew too."

"I haven't seen your father since Dublin. How is he?"

"He is drowning in sorrows, one bar to the next. At least he isn't yelling at me. It feels weird to call him Daddy after knowing he didn't watch out for me."

"For years I called Sheila my Momster, it helped."

"Momster? Really?" Chey laughed so hard she had to sit on the lounge chair.

"Since your engagement, I've taken to calling her Motherzilla."

Chey clutched her middle. "Stop. You are killing me."

After a few minutes Chey calmed. "How could a mom do that?"

"I don't know."

Cheyanne stood and leaned against the railing. "I thought she would get it. With everything in her past. But she is so upset about the wedding."

"Have you decided on your next steps?"

"My in-laws no, they're not my in-laws anymore, have all my stuff that I shipped over. I called them last night. They asked me to stay at their house for the week. Apparently, Chandler hasn't contacted them. But INTERPOL has. Lord Fairfax is furious and more than a little sympathetic to my plight. As weird as it sounds, I think I'm taking their offer. I need to be away from my own parents for a bit."

"And after that?" asked Dana.

"I'm not sure. I have a great job lined up to start next month. Chandler's father found it for me. Honestly, I think I am more excited about the job than I was about the wedding. Since I am not marrying a Brit, I'll need to check, I may need a visa or something. But I'd like to stay and work. And that has nothing to do with not wanting to be anywhere near my mother for the time being."

"Understandable."

Ping.

Chey looked at her phone. She held it up for Dana to read.

CHANDLER: I NEED the ring!

"Is that the first time he's texted?"

"Ya."

"Are you going to give it to him?"

"No. It's a family heirloom. I intend to return it to his mother." Cheyanne tucked her phone into her pocket. "What are your plans? Going back early with mom and dad? Renee, Erin, and Lindie are touring London. No one has heard from Amy-Kate. I think she is in your old dungeon of a room or she got off."

"I wouldn't get on a plane with Sheila in her current mood to save my life."

"Even if you got first class again?"

Dana laughed and shook her head. "I'm staying for a few days. You know I have this thing for Jane Austen. I'm taking the opportunity to go to Bath then down to Lyme Regis. I've always wanted to see the Cobb."

"At least one of us can be romantic."

"You could come with me?"

"No, I am not ready to think about romance. Speaking of—anything more between you and the security officer?"

"Not really. You saw the text when he asked how you were doing, but we haven't had any other conversations since the whole mess when I caught Chandler and Amy-Kate together." The few words that were said when she rebounded didn't count as conversation.

"It's odd. Three security members were there to witness it."

"I thought so too, but it's probably good, or I might have done more than deflect a blow from that jerk."

"Good thing you didn't. I mean, I know you could have taken Chandler any time, any place. He's a wimp compared to the men I've seen you spar with. But I am glad you didn't get put off the ship too. They could have kicked you off, right?"

When McKay wouldn't talk to her at the time, Dana had wondered the same thing. She hadn't been fighting, only defending herself. "I was worried for a hot minute."

"You didn't answer the important question. What about the security guy?"

"I'm going to try to see him once we are home. I just need a moment to talk to him. I don't want to do the whole stalker web search thing though."

Cheyanne leaned forward. "Really? You want to date him?"

"Yes." The confidence in which the answer came out surprised her.

Cheyanne smiled. "Good for you."

"I am really hoping there is something there once he is away from the ship. I mean, he would have to be nice to everyone on board. I'm not sure if he is reciprocating my feelings or not."

"I think there is interest on his part. Even I noticed how he looked at you. Chandler didn't look at me all softy-eyed like that. Next time I get engaged, I'm going to make sure it's for all the right reasons."

"Are you just putting on a brave face? Or are you really not that upset about things?"

"Like I said, I was more excited about my new job and living in the UK. I always knew something was off. I guess I just didn't have enough—I don't know a word for it—flutters?"

Flutters. Dana had definitely been experiencing those. Coming back on ship with Hermione, her heart nearly fluttered right out of her. She never expected to feel that cliche reaction to anyone.

Dana hugged her sister. "I wish this never happened."

"'Next to being married, a girl likes to be crossed in love a little now and then. It is something to think of and gives her a sort of distinction among her companions.' Isn't that what Jane Austen wrote?"

"Yes, she did. Glad to know I have influenced you."

"And I crossed the British Isles. That gives me more than enough distinction." Cheyanne said in a poorly acted British accent.

"You'll be alright then."

"As soon as I get away from the rest of my bridesmaids I will be. They are trying so hard to talk of everything but the wedding. And poor Carlotta leaves the room whenever she sees me, like it's her fault. I like her. We could be friends if she would stop taking on his guilt. Cousin doesn't mean accomplice."

"Have you talked to her?"

"I have, but I think she also feels guilty for taking your place in our room."

"Should I say something? It worked out well for me. Look at this room. I couldn't ask for better. And with the crutches, it was really nice those first few days not to have to put up with any of your noise and have a space small enough I didn't need them."

Chey rolled her eyes. "Put up with my noise? Some big sister you are, valuing peace and quiet over partying."

"A big sister who thinks she needs to come back and visit. Christmas?"

"If you aren't married by then…" her phone buzzed. "Looks like dinner is at the suite. Want to come eat with us?"

"Sure. I'll speak to Carlotta too, maybe that will help her not feel so bad."

Later, as the sun set, Dana took a walk around the track, glad that her ankle gave her no pain. On her second lap, McKay appeared through a nondescript side door.

"Hello, stranger." She slowed her pace.

"What did you think of County Cork?"

"It was nice. I guess I'm just glad this cruise is almost over."

"Do you have plans after?"

She looked out at the sea as to not appear too interested in him, CCTVs were watching. "I don't fly home until Saturday. I'm thinking I'll treat myself to a little Jane Austen tour of England."

"My sister would be jealous."

"She should be. I intend to go sit on the top of the Cobb and watch waves for at least an hour."

"The Cobb is up a long stone wharf thing, isn't it?"

"Points for knowing."

"Let's just say Jen and Mom make sure I've seen all the Jane Austen movies. And I read *Pride and Prejudice*. It wasn't that bad."

Dana laughed. "When do you go home?"

"I have a few things to finish up with at the office, but I believe I will be flying home on Friday. The company is arranging it."

"Have a good flight."

He looked at his feet, almost as if he was unsure of himself. "Would you mind if I contact you when we are both stateside?"

"I'd like that. Do you want my number?"

"That would be helpful. Only I'm still officially a crew member on the ship. And I can't ask you for it."

"I could voluntarily give it to you."

"I'm not supposed to accept it."

"You know my employer. I'll let them know they can give it to you if you call."

"That works."

As they started the next lap, McKay disappeared through an employee only door.

Dana finished walking until she reached the back of the ship. She spied one of the many CCTV cameras. Had he been watching for her, hoping to find a place to talk to her that would not raise suspicions?

She hoped so.

Sixteen

McKay misjudged the time needed at the cruise line's London office with the legal team, both in person and on-line. Apparently, their little discovery of Ian's information sale led to a site on the dark web involving multiple ships and employees. After telling his story for the third time that day, the lead attorney decided there was no more to glean from McKay's testimony.

After the interviews, he completed the rest of his paperwork with HR and received his plane tickets. The Friday afternoon departure gave him a day in London to explore. If only it had been Saturday, he might find Dana. It was a silly idea to locate one tourist out of thousands. After checking into his hotel, he called his mom to give her the flight details and got her voicemail.

He dialed Jen's number next.

Gracie answered. "You're early."

"Hello to you too. Is your mom around?"

Gracie cupped one hand around her mouth. "She's in the bathroom."

"While we wait, can I get your opinion on what I should do for a day in London?"

"Visit a real princess!"

Not possible. "I need to get a special invitation to do that. What else should I do?"

"See a castle?" she asked with less confidence.

"I can do that."

"Will you send me photos?"

"Better yet, I'll bring them home in a couple of days."

His comment earned him a squeal of delight.

Jen took the phone from her daughter. "What did you tell her?"

"That I would bring home photos of a castle in a couple of days."

In the background, he heard a door slam. Jen laughed. "She just ran outside to tell all her friends. She may expect more than a photo of a castle."

"I just called to give you my flight info. I called Mom, but she didn't answer."

"Her phone must still be in the rice. Did you call her landline?"

"No. What happened?"

"Gracie, kiddie-pool, and grandma taking a close-up photo."

McKay laughed with his sister. "Will you tell her my flight information, too?"

Jen wrote the flight times. "You know you could have texted this."

"True, but I wanted to talk over something."

"I'm not Mom, but will I do?"

"Remember that woman I told you about?"

"The bride's sister?"

"Long story short, I know she will be in Lyme Regis on Friday and I didn't get her phone number. I know where she works and can get it from them."

"Awkward."

"Exactly. Which had me thinking of getting a train ticket or renting a car—"

"Yes!" Jen fist pumped the air. "That is the most romantic real-life thing."

"But what if I don't find her?"

"She is going to the Cobb, isn't she?"

"Yes."

"Then you only have to stake out one place."

"Would you think it was creepy?"

"You're my brother, so of course it is creepy. But if I were her and into you—"

"I'd need to change my flight to leave on Saturday."

"Do it. Mom's surgery isn't until Tuesday, so you'll have plenty of time and frankly she'd tell you to miss her surgery for the right woman."

As soon as McKay ended his call he opened his LegacyAir app and changed flights, claiming one of the last open seats on the early Saturday flight. It was the only one he could change to without a fee. After checking the train schedules, he opted for renting a car. Now he just needed an inconspicuous spot to wait without looking like some creeper and scaring other tourists.

The longer he studied satellite maps of Lyme Regis, the more he questioned his sanity. What if she didn't come? What if he couldn't find her? What if someone reported him for suspicious behavior? What if this was the dumbest idea in the history of bad ideas?

Seventeen

THE COBB STRETCHED OUT INTO the calm waters, not the stormy sea in Jane Austen's book. Dana climbed the uneven steps to the sloping top. The wind caught her hair, lifting it into the air. Dana turned to face the wind. It smelled of sea and history. Echoes of thousands of sailors bound for far-off places and the women who waited for them. Of course, Jane hadn't exactly seen or experienced the Lyme Regis sea wall as it stood today, since the last major rebuilding had been a few years after the author's death. Still, the Cobb dated back to the 1300s, before anyone knew the nearby cliffs contained a wealth of dinosaur fossils, giving the town its popularity today.

This was the last stop of her whirlwind Janeite tour of southern England before returning to spend the night in Bath. The afternoon was perfect for her plan to watch the sea and perhaps record a video to send to her father and friends.

Dana walked along the wide top and looked across the water. It was hard to imagine the area as the bustling seaport it had once been. A few tourists passed her. As she planned, Dana sat on the harbor side edge and pulled up the reading app on her phone. She searched for *Persuasion* and found the chapter that occurred in Lyme. Reading an imaginary story in the real place that it occurred seemed somehow fitting. And Brit and Simone would be jealous. Too bad she didn't have the paperback with her because then she could take a selfie of her reading it and send it to them.

"Don't jump."

Startled at the voice that filled too many of her daydreams and interrupted her as she was finishing the chapter, Dana looked down. On the walkway was the last person she expected to see. "McKay? What are you doing here?"

He held up his phone. "Walking along the Cobb and taking a video for Jen and Gracie. *Persuasion* is one of their favorite movies."

"I thought you were supposed to be flying home by now."

"I changed my plans to stay an extra day."

"To film the Cobb?"

"No." He looked up, his eyes searching hers.

He'd come for her. He didn't say it, but the truth of the statement was in his eyes. She needed to get to him. The closest stairs were several yards away. Jumping down to him wasn't such a bad idea, was it? A ten-foot drop to stone. Louisa's fate in the book flashed through Dana's mind. Nope! Bad idea.

"Wait. I'm coming down." She pointed to the closest steps and scooted back from the edge. The steps were narrow and uneven. Dana kept a hand on the wall as she descended. McKay waited at the bottom.

When she reached the second to the last step, he said, "I'll catch you."

Dana paused. "I'm not jumping. I reread the scene not ten minutes ago."

McKay reached up for her waist, his hands closing on either side spreading a warmth through her. "Not much of a jump and I can tell Jen I caught a beautiful woman on the Cobb."

Leaning forward, she placed her hands on his shoulders and allowed McKay's strength to lower her the last foot and a half.

Her friends would swoon if they'd been watching. McKay didn't back up or remove his hands when her feet met the ground. Dana searched his face. Was he trying to make this as romantic of a moment as every Jane Austen fan ever thought it should be?

His eyes lowered to her lips and back to meet hers. An invitation and unspoken question. Dana leaned closer, giving permission and acceptance.

McKay lowered his head and brushed his lips across hers. Once, twice, three times. The third time, she responded, pulling him closer. Letting him know she wanted this as much as he did. He'd come to Lyme Regis for her. He broke the kiss and rested his forehead on hers.

"Two trains and a taxi." Dana's thought slipped out of her mouth.

"What?"

"I was thinking you took two trains and a taxi to find me."

"Actually, I drove. But I would have taken two trains and a taxi if I had to."

Laughter bubbled up in Dana. "I can't believe you're here."

She reached up and kissed him again.

Nearby, someone giggled.

Dana pulled back and looked around his shoulder. A teenage girl was recording them on her phone. She lowered the phone when she realized Dana was looking at her.

"That is the most romantic thing I've ever seen." The girl's Texan accent labeled her as a tourist. "Y'all it will go viral."

McKay turned, keeping one hand on Dana's waist. "I'm glad you found our kiss romantic. We'd rather have kept it private. Would you please delete that video?"

"But it would get so many views."

Dana stepped forward. "I know it would. However, there are people in my life who I don't want to see my first kiss with my new boyfriend on social media before I get home from vacation. And my boss isn't going to like seeing me in a viral video."

The girl frowned. "Fine, I won't post it."

Dana didn't believe her.

From the twitch in McKay's eye, neither did he.

"May I watch you delete it?"

The girl stepped back.

"I have an idea." Dana smiled at the girl. "Download the video to my phone and then delete it. *If* this turns into a forever relationship, we will send you an invitation, complete with an airline ticket, to see us. I'll give you the video back before the wedding and you can stitch it with a kiss you record of us then. And then you can post it with our permission. A guaranteed viral vid for you."

The girl bit her lip. "How do I know you will keep your end of the deal?"

"They same way I know you didn't quickly upload it to the cloud and plan to post it tomorrow. Trust."

The girl eyed them suspiciously. "You might not know if I do."

Dana held out her phone for the girl to see. "Do you recognize this phone?"

The girl's eyes widened. "Where did you get that? It isn't supposed to be out for two more weeks."

"I work with Mr. Ogilvie. I test some of his products. One of the things he will be testing is software that will find images on the web, even in videos. If you post a video of me. I will know in minutes." Dana paused, letting the idea sink in. Colin hadn't invented any such software yet, to her knowledge. She would suggest it the moment she got back to Chicago.

"Ok, I'll drop it to you."

Dana held her phone close to the girl's. The drop only took a few seconds. And then they watched as she deleted the video from her phone.

Dana sent her back her contact information. "I don't like making assumptions, but I guess you are under 18. I want you to talk to your parents before you contact me. Okay?"

"How did you know I'm not eighteen?"

Dana smiled. "Because I was once a teenager, too."

The teen turned to McKay. "I hope you don't break up. She is kinda cool and you let her jump off the Cobb without hitting her head, so she should like you for a while if you don't mess it up. Most guys do, you know?"

Dana bit her tongue to keep from laughing. The girl wasn't wrong, but she wasn't right either.

"I'll do my best."

A couple in their late forties dressed in jeans and t-shirts rushed up. "There you are. We told you not to wander off. Were you bugging these nice people?"

Dana extended her hand. "Dana Knight. We just had a friendly visit. I hope you don't mind. I made a deal with your daughter and if she keeps her end, she might be invited visit us, with you as a chaperone, of course."

"Izzy, you didn't record this nice couple, did you? We've told you not to record strangers." Izzy's mother put a hand on her shoulder.

"But Mom, it was so romantic. I just had to."

The girl's father addressed McKay. "I'm so sorry y'all. We've talked to my daughter about this. I promise she won't post it."

"She already told me she wouldn't," said Dana.

"Sorry." Izzy waved as her mother marched her back down the Cobb.

McKay took Dana's hand and turned toward the end of the seawall. "Why did you make that deal with her? Are you already planning on a wedding?"

"No one ever starts a relationship hoping it will end in shambles. I don't know where this will go. But if it goes somewhere, we have a cool video."

"And if it doesn't?"

"Then I have something to watch and edit things into while I am eating a gallon of chocolate ice cream."

"Do I get a copy?"

"Maybe." Dana pulled him closer to the seawall and checked for tourists with cameras before raising her face for another kiss.

The first drops of rain speckled the rounded rocks on the beach. McKay threaded his fingers with Dana's and pulled her closer. "Looks like we are about to be soaked."

"Where did those clouds come from?" Dana hurried beside him. Both looked at their feet. Most of the rocks were about the size of his fist. It would be easy to misstep, and Dana didn't have her crutches anymore. They hurried toward a line of beach huts where a cement walkway would make their dash for shelter less perilous.

A few steps later, Dana slowed and dropped McKay's hand. She smiled up into the sky. "Why run if we're already soaked?"

She blinked and pushed back her hair.

McKay reached for her. "Isn't this where the couple falling in love kisses in the movies?"

She wrapped her arms around his waist. "Sometimes."

"Why in the rain?"

"It makes good footage?"

McKay brushed a kiss across her lips. She tasted like the sea, wild and unexpected. Unique like the ring in his pocket. It called to him like a mysterious ring of fantasy origin, beckoning him to take it out and put it on her finger, to declare this the first step to the future. Too soon screamed his brain.

Too soon the kisses ended as Dana pulled back with a shiver. "I need to dry off before I catch the bus."

"You're not staying in London?"

"Not tonight. I'm taking the train in the morning." Dana shrugged. "Since there are no scheduled service disruptions, I should get there in plenty of time for my late afternoon flight."

The rain slowed and stopped. The sun came out. Minutes later, people flooded out of the buildings.

"What airline?" He asked.

"Legacy. And you?"

"Same, but I have the early flight. Too bad we aren't on the same one."

"Can you change?"

McKay shook his head, dislodging a drop from his hair, which ran down his cheek. "I already did. I couldn't get my ticket to change to the afternoon one even though it had more empty seats unless I paid to upgrade."

"Do you really want to be on my flight?"

"Unless we are sitting together, I don't see a point."

"If we could sit together?" She tapped something into her phone.

"Only a magician could pull that off."

"Open your phone and show me your ticket?"

McKay did as she asked, knowing it was pointless.

Dana took a photo of his screen and added it to a text message she started. "There. Now we wait."

They turned up the street leading away from the harbor, passing shops and cafés. "Hungry?"

"A little, but my bus will be here in fifteen minutes."

"I can drive you to Bath."

"Where are you staying?"

"Over there." He pointed to an inn he'd found.

"I can't ask you to drive all the way to Bath and back tonight."

His phone rang. McKay looked at the screen, which read "Legacy Air" before answering.

"Hi, this is Britania Johnson from Legacy Airlines. I understand you want to change your booking to coincide with one for Dana Knight?"

This had to be a joke. "Yes, but airlines don't do that."

"Usually not. But Dana is special and I can put you both on the afternoon flight in side-by-side seats in our premium class. Is that acceptable?"

McKay looked to Dana, who was texting on her own phone. "Yes?"

"Perfect. I just need some information to confirm the reservation change."

McKay gave her his frequent flier number and birth date and answered a few more questions.

"You are all set, Mr. Worth. Your LegacyAir app should reflect the new booking. Can you please confirm?"

McKay swiped up to his app. "Yes, the flight change and new seat is there. Thank you."

"Have a wonderful flight."

He thought he heard the woman laugh. He turned to Dana, who was smiling ear to ear. "What just happened?"

"I arranged for a nine-hour date in the friendly skies."

"How?"

"I know someone. And now you have to wake up at dark o'clock to make that drive."

"I could check out of my hotel here in Lyme and stay in Bath." Who cared if he had to pay for the night in both places.

Dana looked at her hands, and an uncomfortable silence sprung up between them.

He recognized his mistake. "In my own room. I wasn't suggesting—" He knew he was blushing and tried to calm his embarrassment. "I know I moved fast with the kiss since we haven't even had a real date."

Relief filled her face. "You could, but won't you lose money?"

"Says the woman who got me an upgrade on an international flight."

"Extra leg room equals a hotel room?"

"Not my point. I could check out. Drive up to Bath. I'll even stay at a different hotel if you wish. Then we can drive into London in the morning together."

"I could get another Sally Lunn bun."

"A what?"

"Hard to explain, but believe me, you'll understand. The restaurant opens at 10:00 for walk-ins. Or we could go over to the

Pump room. Brit says they have absolutely the best blackberry and hibiscus tea ever."

"Brit? As in Britania, the person who just called me?"

"The one and only."

"So we now have a breakfast date, and an airplane date. If we stop and get fish and chips tonight, we will have three dates in one weekend."

"Or one very long one."

"Come on, let's go to Bath. I hope I can find a tourist shop open. My sister will have my head if I don't bring her back something Jane Austen."

"You can always bring back a twenty-pound note since her face is on it. But I am sure you can find something. I believe the shops open at ten too, so if we plan our morning wisely…" She pulled out her phone.

"You can plan in the car. Let's get me checked out and we can find dinner along the way." This was crazy. Spontaneous. Jen and Mom would not believe this. At least his flight time hadn't changed, so he wouldn't have to explain until he got home. If all went well he would give her the ring before they landed at O'Hare. Yes, that would be a much better time.

Eighteen

Dana broke the bun in half. This had been the most perfect first or second date she'd ever experienced. They had breakfast at the Pump room. The tea was as good as Brit claimed. After breakfast, they ran over to the Jane Austen Centre and purchased gifts for Jen and McKay's mom. He said that Gracie was too young to appreciate anything with Colin Firth as Mr. Darcy on it and she had more than enough gifts. They picked up two take away buns from Sally Lunn's as they left town. Neither of them had room for the buns in their carry-ons, so they ate them as McKay drove.

She handed McKay a section spread with clotted cream.

"I hope there isn't a law against eating and driving in the UK."

"No idea. You drive well on the left side of the road."

"You should have seen me going out to Lyme Regis on Thursday afternoon. I haven't driven in six months and between not driving and left-side roads, I thought I was going to be in an accident."

"I'm glad you figured driving out. The trains aren't bad, but a car means much less carting of luggage all over. You know why they drive on the left, don't you?"

His mouth full, McKay shook his head.

"Oxen and knights."

"Huh?"

"In medieval times, knights traveled with their sword arm out to defend themselves, putting their right arm at the center of the road. Obviously in America we were past that era of history, but we were expanding and people got huge covered wagons to do that. Oxen were better for pulling the heavy wagons, but they like to be lead, which most people preferred to do with their right hand, but to see what was coming they wanted to walk in the center of the road and not in the muck at the side of the road. So Americans had their left arm to the center of the road and by the time cars came around both countries did what they were used to doing."

"What about south paws like me?"

"I assume they weren't knights?"

The silence that filled the car as they ate was comfortable. The awkwardness left sometime in the early morning hours. They'd stayed up talking and walking half the night. The Royal Crescent by moonlight was magical. The Assembly rooms were closed of course, but it had been fun thinking of a time when its doors would have been open until the early hours while members of society danced and flirted.

If that was their first date, then this was their second, and so far, it wasn't the mess Brit and Simone predicted. Of course, they had yet to get on the flight.

All too soon, they'd checked in and started the long walk through the terminal. McKay had the privilege of an extra security screening. He finished his screening and sat back down next to her, his arms full of things that didn't fit back into his carry-on.

"That was fun, taking everything out after I worked so hard to get it all in." McKay re-packed his bags.

"Any idea what they found suspicious?"

"Nope. But then they had so many of us come up that it could have been anything."

"We should be boarding any minute so you can relax." Dana covered a yawn.

"That late night is catching up to me, too."

"You don't look tired."

"Ship hours. I am used to getting four hours of sleep here and there."

"Can you sleep on planes?" Dana rolled up a t-shirt for him.

"Usually. Have we run out of things to talk about yet?"

"I hope not. I still don't even know your favorite color."

"Green. I still don't have your phone number."

The speaker overhead crackled and announced their boarding. Dana rolled up another shirt. "We can exchange numbers on the plane. We better get you repacked first."

Finishing just as their boarding section was called, they joined the line.

"Dana, I thought that was you."

She turned her head to see who called her name. "Amy-Kate, what a surprise."

"I should have known you'd be with him. He probably put you up to it." Amy-Kate hoisted her backpack over her shoulder and fell into step behind them. Her designer perfume overwhelmed the crowded space.

"What are you talking about?"

"You and him breaking the rules. No dating crew members. It was all over the place. And you two are sneaking around."

"We only talked on the ship. Nothing inappropriate." Dana scanned her pass.

Amy-Kate put her phone over the scanner. "That's what—"

The gate agent interrupted Amy-Kate mid-sentence. "Miss, it is not your boarding time if you will please step aside and wait until you are called."

"But—"

Dana didn't turn around to see what happened. She took the window seat, leaving McKay the aisle. The premium seats Brit had arranged gave them blessed privacy, with only two seats across so no one else would be in their conversations.

Onboard, she put her backpack under the seat in front of her as McKay stowed his bags above.

"Do you know what Amy-Kate was talking about? I was so careful not to do anything that might get you in trouble. Did the day in Galway cause you problems?"

A muscle twitched in his jaw. "I have an idea, and I promise I am not trying to be evasive, but she has things mostly wrong, and it has to do with Mr. Fairfax and an ongoing investigation."

"An investigation into Chandler? This isn't going to come back on Cheyanne, is it?"

"No. Please don't worry about your sister. She had nothing to do with the problem we discovered."

Dana nodded. Years of training kept her face neutral, but she wasn't a fan of vague secrets, especially when they had something to do with someone she loved. In her industry, the wrong secret could be dangerous.

As dinner was served, Dana replayed the events leading up to the discovery of Chandler and Amy-Kate in the passageway near her room. Questions filled her mind. Ones she'd ignored while consoling her sister.

"Was there anything wrong with my original room?"

McKay looked up from his mini roll he was buttering with a bamboo knife, "No."

"Was it your idea to move me?"

"I opposed it."

He knew about the plan. Dana picked at her asparagus, removing the rosemary leaves. "Why me?"

McKay paused for a long time. "I don't think I can tell you."

Dana stuffed the cheese wedge in her mouth to keep from saying anything until she thought it through. Most of the questions she had would likely fall into the 'unanswerable' category.

"Were any other passengers moved?"

"No. There really had been a problem with that particular cabin when we sailed. They were not able to solve it until we reached Galway, when a part was delivered. No one was disturbed by moving you."

"Oh." Dana finished her meal in silence. Each bite tasted like cardboard in her increasingly dry mouth. After the trays were collected, she excused herself to go to the restroom. Two other people stood in line.

Amy-Kate came up behind her. "I thought with your standards—" she used air quotes. No one used air quotes, making her sister's former friend even more annoying. "—that you wouldn't date someone who lied to you."

"I really don't think you have much to say at this point."

"Entrapment?"

"What do you mean?"

"Mr. Hot Security Dude had to know Chandler and I were there. He must have sent you down the hall hoping you would cause a scene. If you hadn't caught us and started the fight, they couldn't have done anything since we were just kissing. They needed Chandler to assault you. Face it, they used you. And you are so desperate for a guy to like you that you fell for it."

"Why would they do that?" She fought to keep her emotions under wraps.

"Because security realized a crew member must have told Chandler about the spot that no camera could see. They wanted to know if someone was selling information, as if it matters. I got questioned by INTERPOL like I was a criminal. And if you hadn't made a scene, no one would have ever known."

A passenger exited the restroom and squeezed his way past them. Dana waited a moment before continuing.

"Chandler purchased the information about an onboard meeting place where there were no cameras?"

"Yes. Although I wished I had just gotten an extra suite so we could have really been alone. He said he didn't want to be tempted. Not as if we hadn't shared a bed before. But he said we couldn't during the cruise." Amy-Kate rolled her eyes.

Didn't she even care what she had done to Cheyanne? Or that someone else could have purchased that information?

"That is so wrong."

Amy-Kate scoffed. "He loves me more than Cheyanne. She is such a prude. He says he'll come get me as soon as his father forgives him."

The next restroom became available and Dana stepped inside, glad for the privacy to think. Her reflection in the mirror looked composed, but inside her thoughts were seatbelt-yourself-in-and-and-grab-a-sick-bag turbulent.

McKay had offered to walk her back to her room that night. That was the only time since he helped her when she was on her crutches. Officer Alvaro had ordered him to do so the first night. Had he also ordered him the night she found Chandler. She hadn't thought it too odd at the time, as she enjoyed their conversation and his touch. A sting operation with an unknowing accomplice. Why hadn't McKay trusted her enough to include her in the plan? She wouldn't have told Cheyanne if that was what they were worried about.

Dana used a damp paper towel on her face, trying to cool the heat of betrayal rising in her cheeks. Had Officer Alvaro encouraged McKay to stay close to her just for this operation? Was that the real reason she hardly saw him after they caught Chandler?

They had taken advantage of Dana's skills without her knowledge. Hastings Security would have worked with the cruise line. She would have. Trust was essential to a relationship. If under orders, McKay could have apologized even without giving her details. She would have accepted an "I'm sorry." She would have been even more curious, but she would have accepted it. Second date mess? This was way beyond that.

There was only so little he was authorized to tell her. What could he say to Dana in the next six hours that could make things right? Nothing.

McKay scrolled through the movie selection. His finger hovered over each title without really seeing the titles. Avoidance was possibly his best course of action. Although he doubted Dana would say anything that would jeopardize the ongoing investigation, there could be someone on the plane who might overhear. The same protective instinct that made him good at his job now kept him silent. Once he was home, he could contact the cruise line legal department and get permission to disclose more of the details. Once Dana knew why they needed to talk to Chandler, she would understand. She had to.

Dana returned from the restroom. McKay stood so she could get back into her seat. The indicator light showed one of the restrooms was empty. Better to go now before they hit angry seas, or rather, air turbulence. They felt a lot the same. Dana's tight smile indicated they'd already hit them.

When McKay returned to their seats, Dana was leaning against the window, wrapped in a blanket with a sleep mask on. The mask couldn't hide the tension in her jaw. He counted her breaths. She wasn't sleeping.

Still, he wouldn't bother her.

McKay scrolled through the movies again. Why were there so many Hearthfire romances? He found an action movie and settled in for the duration. The first movie ended and he searched for another. Romances. Why so many rom-coms? There was nothing funny about finding someone you were interested in and having it blow up in your face.

Dana "woke" shortly before landing and stretched. "I love the extra leg room, don't you?"

This was how she was going to play it? Polite chatter. It cut deep. "Yes. Did you sleep well?"

"As well as could be expected. Didn't you?" She pointed to his screen.

"No, I couldn't." He was sure she hadn't slept much at all. He wouldn't call her a liar, since her answer could be interpreted in multiple ways. McKay tucked his headphones into his pocket while Dana put away her things.

The flight crew commenced their usual announcements. Then went on to remind passengers to pick up their luggage after customs and ensure it made their connecting flights.

Dana covered a yawn. "I hope the customs line isn't long."

"It usually is. At least you don't have another plane to catch."

The pop and whine of the landing gear vibrated through the plane.

Dana leaned her head back and looked at the ceiling. Her knuckles whitened against the armrest.

"You don't like landings?"

"Not much."

"Anything I can do to distract you?"

She shook her head.

McKay swallowed back a sigh. A continent away, she'd laughed at his jokes, shared his food, and trusted him. Nine hours ago, he was sure she would have let him distract her or at least hold his hand. If only he could tell her more.

The plane touched down with a gentle bump. The queuing of tired passengers began. Few people spoke, including them.

When they reached the terminal, Dana turned, "Thank you for everything. I had a wonderful time."

She ducked into the bathroom.

McKay debated waiting for her. And decided against it—he had a flight to catch. The lines at customs were shorter than the last time he'd flown in. He didn't see Dana again before he was through and out the other side. He should text her goodbye.

Wait. He never got her number.

He waited for a moment for Dana to emerge. The digital clock above the departure board reminded him he couldn't. She could stay inside for hours. Some distances were meant to stay uncrossed.

Nineteen

Without needing to look up, Dana traipsed the path to the train that would take her into the city. Her feet moved automatically through her home airport while her mind replayed the flight. How had she made such a mistake? He used her. Oh, the things she wanted to say. It didn't matter—she never needed to see McKay Worth again. No long-distance relationship would work out.

As she walked, her phone buzzed and pinged as messages, texts, and emails downloaded now that she was no longer in airplane mode. None from McKay apologizing. Of course, they never traded contact information… Just as well. However, there was one from her father.

> Dad: Hey, I know you just flew in but can you come spend the rest of the weekend with me?

> Dana: I would love to. I just landed, so I'll go home, repack and drive on over.

> Dad: You don't need to come tonight. But I have an event tomorrow. I would be honored if you could attend.

> Dana: What?

> Dad: I'm being inducted into the National Blood Donation Hall of Fame.

Dana read the words again. Was there such a thing?

> Dana: Interesting. Like Basketball Hall of Fame?

> Dad: I'll explain when you get here.

Talking with her father would be better than talking with her friends. Brit and Simone would have way too many opinions and way too many questions.

> Dana: I'll be there in a couple of hours. I slept on the plane.

Not a lie. She had fallen asleep at some point. Only to dream of the man sitting next to her.

> Dad: See you soon then.

Dana boarded the train and reviewed the rest of her messages. None of them were urgent. Candace had left instructions about shipping anything Dana needed to the Indiana residence. Most of Dana's personal items sat in boxes in her father's garage. She kept only necessities in her apartment in the Ogilvie penthouse. With Candace and Colin's decision to have the children move to go to school in Indiana, she packed up her possessions before she left for the cruise. Those had been labeled and should've already been taken by the movers to Indiana.

Knowing there would still be frequent trips to Chicago, she left a skeleton wardrobe at the Chicago penthouse. She dropped of her suitcases and throwing a few necessities and her dad's gift into another bag.

She sent off a text to Brit and Simone, letting them know she was going to her father's, since they were expecting her to crash with them for the next couple of days until she needed to drive down to the Ogilvie's.

The only messages from Hastings Security were the automated reminders about hours, substitutions, and PTO.

As promised, she arrived at her father's house only one and a half hours after leaving the airport, a new record. Had McKay made it home? How was his mother doing? She'd never know now.

She parked in the driveway next to Dad's cruiser. Which was probably the best crime deterrent in the neighborhood. The house her grandparents had lived in most of their lives was still well-maintained. But age and lack of multiple bathrooms had relegated the home to a declining neighborhood. Crime on her father's street remained low.

Her father met her in the driveway.

"Were you watching for me?"

"Nah, I was hoping for the pizza delivery guy to show up with a complimentary pie." Dad pulled her into a hug. "How's Chey?"

"Better than expected."

"Give her a hug from me."

"I thought I texted that she stayed in England."

"You did." He took the duffle from her hand and walked her into the house. Leather and a large television replaced the lace doilies and faded prints favored by her grandmother, now living in Florida. But some things never changed. The smell of oregano and garlic filled the air.

"Manicotti?" The familiar scent wrapped around her like a hug. Dana set her backpack down and rushed into the kitchen.

"I figured after two weeks with your mother you could use some comfort food."

"Dad, you are the best." She opened the cupboard and pulled out the old melamine plates. Traces of her grandparents, her father hadn't found cause to replace. "Tell me more about this hall of fame?"

"Apparently there is a National Blood Donation Hall of Fame and I got nominated and accepted."

"For all the blood drives you help with?" It seemed every time she called he was volunteering at another event.

"That and the fact I've donated over ten gallons of whole blood."

Dana paused to stare at her dad. "In vampire math, exactly how much is that? A full course meal with twenty guests?"

Dad set the pan on the trivet and laughed so hard he backed away from the table, holding his side. "I don't think they use vampire math to calculate who gets donations As far as people whom it helps it depends on the need. Statistically that ten gallons would benefit 240 people. Every two seconds, someone in the United States needs a blood transfusion, yet only 3% of people donate. Cancer patients and newborn babies need blood frequently. And internationally? I have no idea. I wish there was more I could do."

"Ten gallons still feels like so much blood."

"It has taken me sixteen years to donate those gallons, in a way it is a lot. Yet, here are many people who have donated more than me. Especially if they calculate in plasma. But when you compare it with how much blood is needed a day, it is the proverbial drop in a bucket."

"Pun intended?" Dana scooped a large serving of Manicotti onto her plate. The cheese stretched in long, perfect strings.

"I didn't catch the pun." Her dad took the serving spoon from her to dish his meal. His wink said otherwise.

"How exactly does this event work? Do you have to drive anywhere?"

"Not far. We are holding it at the blood bank with a special blood drive."

"So instead of a rubber chicken dinner, we are back to providing a vampire banquet?"

"They'll have sandwiches and snacks afterward. More than the normal juice and cookie."

"You should have told me I would have asked my friends to come up."

"You can't donate."

"What?" Dana's fork hovered over her plate, dropping the bite she intended to take. The pasta landed with a soft plop.

"The drive Hasting Security had for their employees was only 50 days ago. You can't donate until a week from Sunday."

"Isn't it close enough?"

Her father shook his head. "It doesn't work like that."

"I guess I'll have to find someplace to donate in a week or so. I can't not donate with my dad joining the hall of fame."

"So, tell me about your trip."

Dana detailed her trip through the rest of dinner, cleaning up, and moving into the living room. She carefully edited out certain details about a certain security officer. Well, as much as possible.

"I brought you a sweater and chocolate." Dana handed her father the bag of goodies.

He set them to the side. "I'm more interested in this Mac character. Your face lights up every time you say his name."

"Dad—" Dana sighed, not able to explain the loss that settled in her soul. "It isn't meant to be."

"So he put a civilian in an awkward position. No one in security would have doubted your capabilities. And if someone is selling information—" He let the implications hang in the air. "You don't need me to spell that out for you."

"It's that they put me in the position to have to find Chandler and Amy-Kate. It's that he didn't apologize. Or trust me enough to include me. The most annoying part is that they used my skills from private security for free in a way. I deserve an apology and an explanation. If they had brought me in officially, they could have given me that. It isn't as if the cruise line hasn't worked with Hastings before."

"After talking with Amy-Kate, did you ask him about it?"

"No." Dana crossed her arms. "It all fits."

"And?"

"I was angry."

"That is my girl. Go big or go home. You never have done things by halves. What you put your mother through redefined 'custody battle.' You made it an all-out war."

"I needed to."

His eyes crinkled with a mixture of affection and exasperation. "Have you ever thought that you could have achieved the same result with a few conversations? I had no idea you were unhappy enough to report Sheila to CPS. You never told me half of what was going on."

Dana raised her brows. It wasn't the first time her father had brought up her over-the-top attitude. "I was ten. And Sheila wasn't much of a mom."

"I agree. Your mother treats you horribly. I'm not saying otherwise. Changing your cabin was low, even for her. However, if you actually spoke to her, the plane could have gone better. I imagine you saw her at the airport, pointed to your foot and said, 'Don't worry, it will be fine.'"

She shifted uncomfortably. "Something like that."

"Sheila may have been looking for you on the plane out of concern, too. Economy tickets and a surgical boot don't seem like a winning combo to me. She may have felt guilty. Maybe they didn't have enough seats in the premier class. When she couldn't find you, she would have been frantic. The fact is you never give her a chance to explain."

Could there be another side to her mother's actions? If so, what did that mean for McKay? "You're saying I should actually talk to Sheila?"

"I wouldn't recommend it for at least a month." A wry smile crossed his face. "I know you have mostly ignored her for the past decade and a half, unless you absolutely had to talk to her. I had hoped you would have had some time to talk things out on this trip."

"I never thought of anything but avoiding her so we didn't upset Chey."

Dad wrapped an arm around Dana's shoulders. "Sheila isn't all bad. I fell in love with her for a few reasons and yes, at eighteen we were too young."

"I've heard this lecture before."

"Apparently it hasn't sunk in yet. And as far as the man you met—well, I thought you were smarter than to let someone go without talking about it."

Dana bit her lip. "I don't have his number."

"Now there is an excuse if I've ever heard one. Don't you work for Colin Ogilvie? How old was he when he hacked the Whitehouse?"

"Pentagon. I think he was twelve."

"There you have it. Ask your boss. Easy peasy."

"Lemon squeezy." If only it were that easy. Colin stayed firmly planted on the ethical side of the fence and he would tell Candace, then the kids would learn of it. They were already far too concerned about her lack of dating. She could try an internet search. She had a name and a town. A yawn interrupted her thoughts.

Dad kissed the top of her head. "Off to bed with you, girl of mine."

"Love ya."

"Same, kid."

"Three full-sized suitcases?" Jen moved a box to make room in the trunk of her car. "Good thing I left Gracie at a friend's. She'd think this was all for her."

McKay put the last suitcase in the back seat. "I guess I accumulated more stuff than I thought. And lots of it is for you, mom, and Gracie."

Jen let a car pass before pulling out. "I'll give you a pass then."

"How did you keep Gracie from coming with you?"

"It wasn't easy, but we need to talk."

"Why?"

Jen turned the wrong direction at the next intersection.

McKay looked out the window in confusion. "I thought we were going to Mom's."

"Mom is in Lutheran."

"The hospital? But her surgery isn't until Tuesday."

"They got her in on late Thurdsay."

"Wait. When you encouraged me to stay, she was in surgery?" His mom could have passed and he wouldn't have known. He had been blissfully playing in Lyme Regis while his mother was in recovery.

"Don't be mad. You know Mom wouldn't want you to pass on love so you could sit in a plastic waiting room chair."

"I would have been better off to come home," he grumbled.

"I thought from the text you sent from Heathrow that things were going well."

"Everything fell apart on the plane. She realized we used her skills without her knowledge to catch our person of interest."

"And she didn't listen to your explanation?"

"Legally, I can't explain much. Then we ran into the woman who was a target of the sting and Dana stopped talking to me." He stifled a yawn. "I'm so frustrated that I couldn't explain. I know whatever she heard was just a half truth."

Jen flipped on her blinker. "You didn't tell me much about Dana. Is she the type of person to jump to conclusions?"

"I guess she is." He hadn't thought so before, but on the plane she—well it was obvious that she didn't care to get all the facts. He yawned again.

"Didn't you sleep on the flight?"

"I couldn't. And we stayed up the night before walking around Bath."

"So, neither of you had much sleep?"

"No. She was pretending to sleep and I didn't want to sleep in case she woke up and I missed my chance to explain." He looked up at the large hospital wondering which room his mother was in. "Enough about me. What happened with mom?"

His sister found a parking space in the visitors' lot. "They had a cancellation, and the surgeon moved up her surgery."

"And?"

Jen exited the car without answering.

McKay fumbled with his seatbelt. By the time he exited the car, his sister was several paces ahead of him. "Jen?"

She shook her head and walked faster. McKay ran a hand over his short hair. He could grow it out now and maybe add a beard. Why was he thinking that when his mother was in the hospital? "Jen, wait up."

The hospital doors swooshed open. McKay finally caught up with his sister at the elevator bank. "Tell me what is going on."

"I don't know completely. Mom wanted to tell us what they found when we were together." She pushed the numbered button for their mom's floor.

They rode the elevator in silence. His sister had to know more than she was telling. Jen wouldn't look at him. How bad was it? McKay followed his sister to the room, relieved to find his mother was not in ICU.

Still, her face was pale and pinched. She held out her hand to McKay as he entered the room. "There you are. How was your flight?"

"A bit bumpy." Metaphorically speaking. Mom would get the details out of him at some point. "How are you?"

"If I told you 'great,' would you believe me?" Mother's words came out slow and measured, negating any humor she infused into her question.

"No."

"What if I tell you I am doing better than expected."

"Also not reassuring."

Mom looked at Jen. "Hard to get something past him."

Jen crossed her arms. "You've kept me in suspense for two days. Telling the doctor he couldn't communicate with me was hardly fair."

"I don't see it that way. You both knew the cancer had come for a return visit and that this time it was bad. The surgery is only to buy me some time and to decide if other interventions are needed. After counseling with my oncologist, I am taking one round of chemo in hopes of living through this Christmas."

Jen gasped.

Just over six months. He needed to sit, but the chair was too far from his mother's side. McKay reached for his mother's hand. She took his, but her grip was less than that of a young child's.

"I've been here before and done this whole cancer treatment regiment. I'll start the treatment the week after Gracie's trip to the park. I wanted to go and perhaps ride some of the rides without being sick. My doctor says I shouldn't, so we will see. No promises to Gracie yet. I am going to do as much as I can in my last few months."

McKay wanted to protest. There had to be something more that could be done. "But—"

His mother cut him off with a look. "I got a few more years than we planned on last time. I know neither of you is ready. No one ever is. Put away those long faces. I am in no mood to lecture you or hear alternative plans."

McKay sat in silence, a helplessness he couldn't battle blanketed him. He'd known since he got the news that this would be the end, but until now he hadn't felt the enormity of it.

"If you are going to stare at me like I am already gone, I'll page the doctor and have him put the mass he removed back in. Think of this as a blessing. You know what to plan on and thanks to the fact this isn't the first time, all my affairs are in order, so we can not be bothered by the pesky little details."

"Why didn't you consult with us?" asked Jen.

"Because we would have come to the same conclusion. Now if you'll excuse me, the painkiller makes me tired. I'll see you tomorrow and then McKay can tell me all about his new love. I want to be alert for the story." Mom's voice faded, while she closed her eyes as she finished speaking.

The only sound in the room was the faint beep of the heart monitor. Jen studied it as only a nurse could. She nodded and left the room. McKay followed.

In the car Jen didn't turn on the ignition. "I suspected this, but hearing her say it. Christmas. Can you stay that long?"

"I didn't sign a new contract which means I have as long as I want." The last three days he'd toyed with the idea of staying on land. He'd daydreamed about settling down, having a family of his own. But in the background, his children had a grandmother. Tomorrow he would have to lie. He never lied to Mom. Well, there was that incident with the hammer and the window, but he was nine. This lie would have to be convincing.

Twenty

Dana's apartment was absurdly quiet. For the first time since she started this job, the door leading to the Ogilvie's was locked from their side. A problem she hadn't anticipated as she always used their laundry room. She texted Brit and Simone.

> Dana: Can I use your washer and dryer? I'm locked out of the Ogilvie's.

Minutes passed before she got a response.

> Brit: Sure. Simone is on a flight and I won't be back until 6 or so. I'll tell Javier and ask him to let you in.

> Dana: Thanks.

The head of building security, Javier, also worked for Hastings. Dana opened the app and sent him a direct message before she gathered her laundry and headed to the elevator.

At Brit's floor, the door opened. Javier leaned against the opposite wall. "You could have asked to use my laundry, you know."

"I don't know your new roommate and didn't think he'd take kindly to having a stranger in there."

"I don't have one yet. Hastings hasn't hired anyone new. With the Ogilvies moving to Indiana, they are playing musical chairs or apartments with the security teams." He stopped in front of Brit's door and tapped his phone to unlock the door. "Are you going to go in and out?"

"No, I brought a book and I have enough laundry to keep me busy until Brit gets home."

"Text me if you do and I'll give you access until later." He grinned. Javier had that magnetic charm that made most women swoon.

Dana considered herself immune to it, but it lifted her spirits. "You could have given me access from wherever you were."

"And miss seeing you? I understand there is a love interest to talk about."

"How could I be in love with anyone but you?" The familiar banter comforted her. "But I have news Brit and Simone haven't heard yet."

"Really? Tell."

"They inducted my father into the Blood Donation Hall of Fame yesterday. Now you know something they don't, which should make your day."

"You know me too well."

"Which is why I don't succumb to your charms." Dana set her laundry down inside the door. "See you later."

Sometime between changing the whites and starting the darks, Dana fell asleep on the couch. She woke to Brit shutting the front door. Dana sat up and stretched.

Brit set her purse on the table. "Now I know why you didn't answer your text about what I should pick up for dinner."

"I guess I still have jet lag."

"Simone should be here in—" Brit checked her watch "—45 minutes. I put in an order for dinner. I figured I couldn't go wrong with Italian, especially if I ordered Cannoli. The hard part is going to be not asking you about anything until Simone gets here."

"I'll go change my laundry, then we can't talk for a moment."

"That works. I'll change clothes. If we are both very slow…"

"Then we can talk about Javier personally letting me into the apartment when he could have done that from his desk."

"Really? Simone isn't here for him to flirt with. He had to know that."

"You know Javier. Flirting is a competitive sport. He has to practice. He just forgets I am immune to his charms." Dana went to change her laundry.

After another round of chit chat, Simone arrived with the promised take out. "Please tell me you didn't talk about your trip or especially your Captain Wentworth."

"No, you only missed an update on my father's induction into the Blood Donation Hall of Fame. He's given over ten gallons in his life and he has volunteered for the past fourteen years."

"Wow. That is a lot." Simone kicked off her shoes. "Now tell us what we've been waiting for. Do you have pictures?"

Dana thought of the video and her cheeks flamed.

Brit raised a brow. "What kind of photos do you have?"

"I have a video. And well, since it's over, I can eat ice cream and watch it." Dana handed over her phone rather than hear her friends beg her to see.

Simone fanned herself dramatically as she rewatched the video. "And why is this over?"

"Because I was stupid." As they ate, Dana told them the story of Chandler and Amy-Kate and what Amy-Kate said on the plane.

Brit set aside her empty plate. "And you didn't ask him to explain more?"

"No."

"Why haven't you texted him for an explanation?"

"I don't have his number." Dana put up a hand. "I found his social media—"

"What?" asked Simone.

"So many women tagged him in photos."

Brit tapped on her phone. "Oh my, that is a lot of women. Although I don't think the senior citizen crowd counts as competition."

Dana took her phone back. "I was probably just another cruise ship COW."

"COW?"

"Crush of the week. A term I learned from Chey's friends. Only this time he was ordered to keep me around so they could have their stupid sting and talk with Chandler."

"I don't know about that. That was some kiss." Brit fanned herself. "That was too real to be following orders."

"He can kiss." Dana sighed. Two days of second guessing herself, and that was the one fact that didn't change. She'd enjoyed his kiss far above any other in her life. She needed to change the subject. "Hey, I brought you chocolate. We can finally compare Irish Cadbury to English Cadbury."

"Seriously, you're giving up?" asked Brit.

"Where is your inner Ann Elliot? You should be running through the streets of Fort Wayne searching for him!" Simone's encouragement would've been camera worthy if it weren't for the little piece of cannoli stuck to her upper lip.

Dana pointed to her laundry baskets. "Work? I just took more than two weeks off. I can't exactly take another road trip right now."

Brit leaned forward. "Are you trying to tell me you will not have a day or two off anytime in the next couple of weeks?"

Dana rolled her eyes. "Of course I will. Fort Wayne may not be Chicago, but it's plenty big and I'm hardly likely to find him Ann Elliott style since I don't know where to look."

"Your internet search didn't bring up an address?" asked Simone.

"No, but that's not surprising, considering that he's been living on a ship for the last several years." She loved her two friends dearly, but they needed to drop this inquisition.

"What about his mom or sister?" pressed Simone.

"I have some possibilities for his mom, but with her cancer, I hardly want to bother her." The mention of cancer dampened the conversation.

Brit picked up the remote. "How about we binge a movie and try that chocolate?"

"One condition, not *Persuasion*." Dana couldn't risk seeing any movie that highlighted the places she'd been with McKay.

Twenty-one

McKay helped his mother sit up on her couch. Each movement brought strain to her face.

"Stop fussing over me." She swatted at his hovering hands.

"That is a no go. You are the entire reason I came home. I'll fuss all I want to."

"If you are going to fuss, then the least you can do is entertain me and tell me about the woman." Her eyes sparkled with interest—the first real animation he'd seen since they arrived home that morning.

"I told you the whole story." In the end, lying hadn't been an option. Mom got more truth than the cruise line lawyers were likely to want her to have. "She walked off of the plane and out of my life."

"But you like her?"

McKay sat in the chair opposite of the couch. "I liked her a lot."

More than like.

More than a lot.

He'd been on board with the whole marriage idea. Even if it was just a ruse to keep Dana off of social media.

"Have you texted, or snapped, or whatever you do?"

"I don't have her number and she isn't on any social media. She works in personal protection in Chicago. I think she has a high-profile client." A client with children. He'd narrowed it down to three, not that it did him any good. He wouldn't get within 100 yards of them.

"Can you leave a number at her work?"

"Probably not." He didn't dare. The last thing he needed was to be on Hastings Security's radar. Dana had been correct that it was unprofessional for them to use her, knowing that she was a security professional. He should have pushed to contact Hastings over the matter, bringing in Dana from the start. "It's okay, really. Between her work and the distance, it would have been difficult to continue the relationship for long."

His mother's knowing look—its power undiminished by the cancer—cut straight through his excuses. "I don't believe you. You could have found a way if you wanted to."

They had. There had been a few vague ideas on her side since her schedule varied. It would have been so much easier if they'd exchanged numbers. "We could have, but it doesn't matter now. Do you want anything to eat?"

"No, I want to pretend for one minute that you had her number and hear all about her."

To please his mother, McKay told the story again, with as much detail as he dared. When he talked about the Claddagh rings, he paused.

"Did you go back and get her one?"

"I did. It was a silly thought. She is the same size as you. You can have Dana's too." Pretending that he always intended it for his mother would be easier than having it sit on his nightstand and mocking him.

Mom shook her head. "I think you are giving up too easily."

"What am I supposed to do?"

"Email her."

"I don't have her address."

"Nonsense. Even I know that most employers use a name variant, try Dana dot Knight at Hastings Security or D dot Knight. Worst case, it bounces."

"Or it goes into a black hole and I never know if she got it or not, or if she is ignoring it." The thought of Dana deliberately ignoring his message twisted something in his chest.

"At least you would have tried. You mentioned talking to her boss. You could—"

"No. Not contacting Hastings. I'd have to explain, and the cruise line should have hired her. I don't think I should be the one to tell them."

"I guess it is your loss." Mom picked up the remote and turned on the TV. "Would you mind getting me a sandwich?"

McKay went into the kitchen. Mom had been less than subtle about ending the conversation where she did. She wanted him to stew and think about contacting Dana. The thought was completely unnecessary, as he'd been stewing for days. The rose gold ring would not let him forget what he gave up.

On her way out of town, Dana stopped at Hastings Security. The familiar glass doors greeted her—her reflection was not nearly as cheerful.

ZoElle appeared from her office, waddling slightly, one hand resting on her rounded belly. "Glad you stopped by."

"I needed to grab a couple of things out of my gym locker. And I believe Chris and Tian had a package delivered here?"

"Oh, yes." ZoElle pointed to a large box near reception. "You'll forgive me if I don't help you with that." She patted her belly with a rueful smile.

Dana laughed. "I wouldn't let you if you tried."

"Do you have a minute to chat?" ZoElle's tone carried that particular note that meant this wasn't really a question.

"Sure," Dana said hesitantly, following ZoElle into her office. The room still smelled faintly of ginger.

ZoElle shut the door and eased into her chair.

"Is something wrong?" Dana asked.

"That's what I would like you to tell me."

"What do you mean?"

"Rumor has it that our little Hastings app fiasco brought you to the attention of a handsome officer aboard ship." ZoElle's eyes sparkled with interest.

"How did you hear that?"

"Javier." ZoElle leaned back, adjusting a cushion behind her. "But I haven't heard the rest of the story."

"Just a minute. You're living for gossip now?"

"Oh, please, give me something," ZoElle said, rubbing her back. "I need a distraction from running to the bathroom every twenty minutes and being kicked in the diaphragm."

"Yes, I met someone. But..." Dana trailed off, unsure how to explain the complicated tangle of emotions the cruise had left her with.

"But what?"

"There's not a lot to tell that you haven't heard already."

"I think there is." ZoElle handed her tablet to Dana. "I received this email this morning."

"It's not addressed to me." Dana tried to hand the tablet back, but ZoElle's expression stopped her.

"I think you should read it."

ZoElle Hastings,

I doubt you remember me. I was one of the security members on board your infamous Panama cruise and, more recently, was on a cruise around Ireland with Dana Knight.

I'm writing to apologize to Hastings Security and, hopefully, to Dana herself.

We had an incident that was handled poorly, both by myself and, I feel, by my senior officer. Unfortunately, Dana was caught in the middle.

After reviewing what happened, I feel… I wish that I was at liberty to say more. However, I believe the cruise line owes Hastings Security—and specifically Dana—an apology.

I have spoken to my former superiors about this, and sadly, it will not happen.

My biggest regret is that I did not disobey orders and take Dana into my confidence.

Her role in what happened enabled us to take down an operation that spanned more than one cruise line— an operation that, if left unchecked, could have hurt many people.

Dana once told me that if I wanted her phone number, I should contact Hastings. I doubt she would trust me with that information now, but if you will, please pass on my sincerest apologies.

Thank you,

McKay Worth

Dana handed back the tablet, her hands slightly unsteady. "Well?" ZoElle's voice was gentle. "What happened?"

Dana described, as briefly as possible, the altercation with Chandler and what she'd learned from Amy-Kate. Speaking it aloud made her realize how much of her anger stemmed from hurt—not at being used in the investigation, but at feeling McKay hadn't trusted her enough to include her.

"Wow," ZoElle picked up a ginger cookie. "Do you want one? I don't need them anymore but I can't stop eating them."

Dana took a cookie to give her a moment to process.

ZoElle brushed a crumb off of her blouse. "That is an unexpected twist to your cruise, to say the least. So, may I pass on your phone number?"

Dana bit her lip. "I'm not sure I'm ready to talk with him. I mean, I understand why he did what he did, and he was following orders, but—"

"But you feel you still can't trust him?"

"Something like that." Though even as she said it, Dana wondered if she was being fair. After all, hadn't she jumped to conclusions without giving him a chance to explain? Dad had pointed out the same things.

ZoElle tapped a couple of keys on her tablet. "There, I forwarded the email to you. Now you have his email address, and you can do anything you want with it."

"Thanks, I think."

"Do you need to grab any snacks from the break room for your drive?"

"No, I'm pretty well stocked."

"Oh, please take some. Alan's been getting me the weirdest things, and I really want them gone. The break room looks like a convenience store exploded."

Dana laughed. "Well, if you have some of those little cookies."

"I'm pretty sure there's a case, or three. Alan thinks I need to eat enough for an army."

The four-hour drive to Robyn's Place stretched ahead of Dana, giving her plenty of time to think. She'd loaded her phone with audiobooks, but her mind would keep circling back to McKay's email.

To email or not to email—that was the question.

It weighed on her every bit as much as Hamlet's famous line.

Alan Hastings's email wasn't what McKay expected—though honestly, he wasn't sure what he had expected. The message was short and businesslike, thanking McKay for his integrity in contacting them while acknowledging that his instinct to follow orders wasn't entirely wrong. Professional. Cordial. Empty.

Most disappointing was the complete absence of any mention of Dana. Would Hastings Security pass on his message? He might never know. The uncertainty gnawed at him worse than seasickness in a hurricane.

After plugging his phone into the charger, he set his phone down with more force than necessary on his nightstand. The ring box from Galway sat there, mocking him. Frustrated, he yanked open the drawer and dumped the box in. At least he wouldn't have to look at it anymore, wouldn't have to remember the way Dana's eyes had lit up in that jewelry shop, or how she'd blushed when the shopkeeper assumed they were together.

Other than at bedtime, he kept himself busy enough that he hardly missed Dana—except when his mother mentioned her, which happened with increasing frequency. Or when Gracie asked if there were any more little lambs hidden in his suitcases. Or when he took his mother to the hospital and saw someone leaving on crutches, remembering how Dana had managed hers with surprising grace.

He searched the internet again. No Dana Knight. Was it even possible for a twenty-something-year-old woman to be that absent from the internet? Weren't women practically required to have Instagram accounts full of food photos and sunset shots? But then again, she worked in personal security. Maybe staying off social media was part of her job.

The baby monitor on his nightstand crackled—a new addition since his mother's surgery left her weaker than expected. He checked to make sure the other end in his mother's room was working properly, and listened to her steady breathing for a moment. Then he punched his pillow and attempted to sleep, trying not to think about how different his night had been in Bath, walking the lamp-lit streets with Dana until dawn threatened.

Twenty-two

A BLACK WALNUT TREE SHADED the path to the bungalow that was to be Dana's shared residence. With summer, the Ogilvies hired a third personal protection "nanny" for the children, allowing all to keep reasonable hours. The bunkhouse cottage also gave increased privacy to the family, since the employees were not under the same roof. All and all, Dana counted it a win.

Dana carried her suitcase into her room. As the texts from the rest of the detail promised, there wasn't a bad bedroom in the house. Each came with its own ensuite bathroom, and a sitting room, a luxury she hadn't expected.

Dana pushed open the window, letting in the sweet Indiana breeze. Behind the decorative shutters, she discovered a blackout shade—perfect for sleeping off night shifts. Candace Ogilvie really had thought of everything. This job would spoil her for all other work.

Which was the point. Candace and Colin wanted stability in their children's lives, which included the necessary protection needed by a billionaire's child. Alan Hastings met with the school district last month on Candace's quest to make sure her children's lives were as normal as possible. Eventually, their classmates would figure out the children's father designed their favorite electronics, but hopefully not until after they had made good friends.

After unpacking, Dana checked the Hastings App. The family was at Robyn's Place. Now was a good time to familiarize herself with the home.

She found Chris Johnson in the small security office off the garage and checked in.

"I thought you were working at Robyn's Place."

"I have a cough. Until it's confirmed to be allergies, I'm on family detail." Chris shrugged. With many of Robyn's Place's future guests being immunocompromised, health protocols were necessarily strict.

"Is it ready for the opening?"

"I think so. The first group comes next week. The foundation picked children that all live within a couple of hours drive and who are relatively healthy for the first round. Still, my cough is enough to bench me from today's walkthrough."

"Speaking of walkthrough, I wanted to look in the residence. I haven't seen it since it was completed."

"You have the pass codes?"

"Yes."

Chris thrummed his fingers on the desk. Something was bothering him.

"What?"

"Trying to decide if I should warn you about Colin's new AI."

"New voice?"

"Nope. New and updated programming. I swear it can read your thoughts. Last night, it told me the exact time Tian's flight would land and what I should have prepared for dinner. Even told me to take her flowers."

"That has to be a joke. Colin programmed it."

"He claims he had nothing to do with it. Good luck getting past her."

Dana entered the main residence. The AI's voice confirmed her access and smoothly recited her schedule for the next two days. Not wishing to be on its bad side—just in case Chris wasn't exaggerating—Dana thanked the computer.

"Peter's new hiding place for his elephant is the cubby under the stairs," the AI informed her. "I will alert you if he moves it."

"Thank you."

"It is my opinion that you blew it with the ship's officer. I agree with Tian."

Dana froze. The AI really did know everything. Or it was an exceptionally good eavesdropper. "Noted."

"According to my research, you should make a grand gesture. Unfortunately, I cannot help you locate the Officer. My ethics contract limits my research model."

A contract that apparently didn't include being nosey or listening to conversations. Tian must have discussed the Officer Worth situation within the AI's hearing. Dana wondered if the AI's ethics contract had a clause about meddling in romance—and if not, whether she should suggest one to Colin.

"Just four more days, Uncle Mac!" Gracie bounded into the house, her excitement filling the room.

"Are you all packed yet?"

"Everything except my toothbrush. Mommy won't let me pack that yet."

She danced across the room, stopping in front of her grandmother to give her a gentle hug. "How are you feeling today, Grandma?"

"Just fine, sweetheart."

"I wish you could come with us to Robyn's Place."

"Ah, but there are only tickets for three people, and I think Uncle Mac is a better person to go."

They'd been hiding the truth from Gracie that the recovery was slower than everyone liked. Mom wouldn't last the drive over.

"I'll tell you all about it. Did you know they have a roller coaster inside?" Gracie threw her arms out wide, indicating its size.

"Yes, I believe you've told me that before."

Jen entered through the front door, a casserole in her hands and a grocery bag on her arm.

McKay held out his hand to take something. "I see someone's a little excited."

"A little?" Jen handed over the grocery bag. "You would think we had an all-expense-paid trip to Florida with her enthusiasm."

"Ah, but this is better."

"I know. I won't have to worry about all the people and all the germs."

"I can't believe I'm letting her go to public school this fall."

"It will be good for her," said Mom.

"I know. I still, worry."

Seeing the bag contained books, McKay set it down on the end table. "Does the doctor?"

"No, thank heavens." Jen carried the casserole into the kitchen. "I brought your favorite chicken and rice, Mom. I'm sure Mac's been eating you out of house and home."

His mother chuckled. "Not as much as you think. He seems to have lost his appetite."

Jen reappeared in the doorway. "Is that what men do when they've lost the love of their life?"

McKay rolled his eyes, though the words hit closer to home than he cared to admit.

"What love of your life, Uncle Mac? What love?"

"You!" He picked up Gracie and swung her around, grateful for the distraction. The movement reminded him of helping Dana down from the Cobb, and he set Gracie down perhaps a bit too quickly.

"You haven't lost me."

McKay gave her another hug. "Well, then, your mother must be wrong."

"Are you two staying for dinner, Jen?" asked his mother.

"Yes, I have time before my shift. Are you sure you can handle Gracie and Mac?"

"Gracie's easy. She cleans up after herself."

"Hey, I do too," said McKay, though his room still held half packed suitcases.

Jen sat down next to McKay's computer, glancing at the screen. "Hastings Security? Are you looking for new jobs?"

His heart quickened at the name on the screen. "I don't know if they would hire me, but they are the security for Robyn's Place, and it's close enough that I would be nearby."

"You're not going back to the ship?"

McKay shook his head. "No, I've decided not to renew my contract with them."

"Because of the thing?" Jen carefully avoided mentioning Dana's name.

"Partially. I also think it's just time to be on land, to be around for all the things that I miss." *Like the chance to build something real with someone special that lasts more than two weeks.*

"I hope you're not staying for my sake," scolded his mother.

"No, Mom. It's time to be home." How long it would feel like home was another issue.

"Any other job leads?" asked Jen.

"I'm not looking that seriously yet." He had his hands full, taking care of Mom. Once things changed, he could figure out the next step. Maybe he would apply to Hastings, if no other reason than to go to Chicago and have a chance of finding Dana.

"Slow down, Chey. What's wrong?"

"Sorry," Chey's voice came in a little gasp over the phone. "I'm just really worried about Mom."

"Why? What happened?" Dana sat on the end of her bed.

"I think Dad left her. She was such a mess. I've never seen her like—"

Mitchell left? Unbelievable. They seemed fine on the cruise. "Like what, Chey?"

"Just upset. Just crying and blaming herself. We knew she knew about Chandler's affair before the wedding, but she was just telling me all these things and how everything she's done in her life was wrong. I was almost afraid to let her off at Heathrow."

"She's flying to Chicago?"

"Yes. Dad left yesterday. Just got in a taxi and left."

"What do you want me to do?"

"Her flight lands in—" Chey paused "—six hours. Is there any way you can be in Chicago to pick her up?"

Dana looked at her schedule. If she switched one shift, she could do it. "Yes, I can go."

"I hate to ask this of you, Dana. I know you two don't get along, but I'm really worried about her."

"I've been thinking a lot about our mother since I returned from England. I want to see her and see if we can start to move forward." Dana pulled out her go bag and added an extra t-shirt, better for the summer heat.

"Really? That would be so nice." The relief in Chey's voice was palpable.

"I'll leave as soon as I talk to Chris about a schedule change. Maybe twenty minutes."

"Call me later?"

"I will. Hugs!"

The drive from Indiana to O'Hare reminded Dana why she always took the train out to the airport—parking was an absolute nightmare. She entered the terminal and checked the boards. Her mother's plane had landed only five minutes prior. She'd need a good half hour, if not more, to clear customs.

Dana found a seat outside the customs exit and checked her phone. There were texts from Brit and Simone, welcoming her to crash at their apartment tonight. Dana wasn't sure how the afternoon was going to go, but she knew she would not be up for the four-hour drive back.

Every few minutes, she looked up to see if Sheila had arrived. Her phone pinged with a notification from her weather app. A storm was coming in.

"What are you doing here?"

"Mother." Dana forced a smile.

Sheila's eyes softened.

"I came to get you. Chey's worried."

"Oh, posh. She doesn't need to be worried. I can take a cab."

"I'm here. I have my car. Why don't I drive you home? It'll be much faster." Dana reached for the suitcase.

"Okay. With all my suitcases, I could use the help." Her mother had obviously picked up an extra suitcase somewhere along the way.

Once in the car, Dana searched for something to say. "I didn't think you would still have been in England."

"Oh, we came home right after the wedding was cancelled. Then we went back. Didn't Cheyanne tell you?"

"She said Mitchell left you."

"Yes. It's all my fault. I'm too needy. I'm not one of those women who can live without a man to provide for her. I never have been a good employee. I know it's no excuse. I would have been a better woman if I was only strong like you."

"Strong like me?" Dana inhaled. No stench of alcohol.

"You stood up for yourself. You stood up to me from the very start. I didn't know what to do with you. I dragged you through some pretty horrid things. You were a little girl. It wasn't your fault, even if I blamed you."

Dana wasn't about to question what specifically wasn't her fault. "I don't talk to you enough. And sometimes I think that makes things worse."

"Do you know how worried I was when I saw you at O'Hare when we were leaving for Chey's cruise? You were on crutches. Crutches! And you hadn't even told me."

"I kind of figured you wouldn't care. I told Chey."

"I know. Then when I couldn't find you on the plane—"

"You got a little upset."

"Embarrassingly so." Sheila scoffed.

Dana wondered if she should tell her father he was right. She turned onto the suburban street and stopped in front of the large house.

"Do you want to come in for a minute?" asked Sheila.

"Sure. You'll need help with those bags anyway."

Sheila punched in the code for the alarm. The house was silent.

Sheila walked in the direction of her bedroom. Unsure what to do, Dana took the suitcases only as far as the bedroom door. Sheila came out with tears rolling down her face.

"He did. He left me. What am I going to do?"

Sheila threw herself into Dana's arms.

Dana let her cry, reminding herself that this was for Cheyanne's sake. "Will you be okay here tonight?"

Sheila sniffed. "I suppose so. All my things are here. And the dog sitter is going to deliver my dogs in an hour. I really should be here for them."

Dana guided her mother over to the couch.

"Are you going to be alright? Do I need to call somebody for you?"

"No, I'll be fine."

"Chey's really worried that you might hurt yourself."

"No, the only person I'm going to hurt is Mitchell." Sheila straightened her shoulders. "Do you know why he really left me?"

Dana shrugged.

"I'm surprised, considering your relationship with the security officer."

Not going there. "Why did he leave?"

"He's running from INTERPOL."

That was the last guess Dana would have had. "INTERPOL? Why?"

"Apparently, he had this side business where employees of hotels, casinos, and cruise lines would sell information. He orchestrated it all. Do you know how many people—women—could have been hurt? How many thefts could have happened?"

Chandler. Amy-Kate. The CCTV.

Her stepfather was behind it? McKay would never believe that. Of course, she couldn't tell McKay. But still. "So, you're telling me that Cheyanne's dad is behind the people that allowed Chandler to buy information so he could meet up with Amy-Kate and cheat with her during the bachelorette?"

"I thought he was just upset about the wedding being off, which was why he was drinking so much on the ship." Sheila shook her head." I always choose the wrong men. The only time I chose right was your father."

"But you've been with Chey's dad for so long."

"Yes, because, like I said, I'm not a strong woman. I need somebody."

"Mom, do you have a counselor or a therapist we could call?"

"Oh, of course I do, dear. Why didn't I think of that?"

Sheila whipped out her phone and made a call. The therapist could see her in an hour.

"You'll stay to let the dogs in?"

"Sure."

Dana made herself as useful as possible, spending most of the time with the dogs while she waited for her mother to return.

When Sheila returned, she was all smiles. She gave Dana a hug. "Thank you. Thank you for coming. An apology for everything sounds hollow, but maybe we could try to be friends."

"I think I'd like that, Mom."

Sheila dropped her purse on the counter and opened her phone. "You have that money app, don't you? The one I can send you money from my bank account?"

"Yes."

"Good."

Her mom tapped the phone. Dana's phone pinged. A \$2,000 deposit.

"I think I owe you much more than that for the cruise and things. But that is the sending limit."

"Thanks, Mom."

"And don't worry about me. I'll be alright. I'm going to text your sister, and maybe I'll go visit my sister. Sisters are such a wonderful thing."

Dana left her mother's house somewhat perplexed yet lightened.

She arrived at Brit and Simone's later than planned, and they were both waiting up for her with their new favorite chocolate ice cream."

"How did things go with your mom?" asked Brit.

"Shocking." Dana glossed over most of the details as she told them about the tentative reconciliation she had with her mother.

"I can't believe she took responsibility," said Simone.

"Me either." Dana finished the last of her dessert.

"Maybe now you should take some responsibility," said Brit.

Simone tried to hush her roommate.

"What do you mean?"

"You told us you had his email. You haven't contacted him yet. Don't you think you owe him an apology?"

"But he owes me one."

Brit held up her hand. "No, you owe him one for not giving him a chance to explain."

Dana retired to the spare room and pulled out her phone.

Brit was right.

It was a day for reconciliation.

Twenty-three

OVER THE YEARS, MCKAY HAD visited amusement parks all over the world. He'd worried Robyn's Place couldn't compete. He'd been wrong.

For one, it wasn't crowded—no more than ten people in any line. His security training automatically kicked in as he counted: roughly a hundred visitors, not including staff. Everyone stayed in family groupings, creating an intimate atmosphere unlike any park he'd experienced. The space rivaled the Astrodome in size, with retractable roof panels currently pulled back to allow in streams of summer sunlight.

Their check-in at the private hotel last night had been thorough but efficient. The wristbands they wore were coded to match Gracie's, making family units easily identifiable—a security measure disguised as convenience. Each guest underwent a quick fever scan, reminding him that this wasn't just any theme park. This was a haven for children like Gracie.

A man in an elaborate pirate costume intercepted them, his theatrical voice booming. "Ahoy there, Gracie!"

Gracie's eyes lit up at hearing her name—another bit of carefully programmed magic that made the place special.

"Have you been to my pirate ship today? We're going to sail the seven seas!"

"My Uncle Mac used to really sail the seven seas, but I'm coming to your pirate ship too!"

"Ah, you make sure you do that!"

The pirate spoke to Jen for a moment before moving on.

"Did you ever meet a pirate, Uncle Mac?"

"I can't say that I have," McKay replied, though his mind flashed to some questionable characters he'd encountered in various ports.

"So, what's next on your list?" Mac asked.

Jen consulted her phone. "Looks like our tickets are next for the racecourse."

The attraction queues were perfectly timed to eliminate lines and put only one or two families on a ride at once.

"Do you think Uncle Mac can beat me at driving?" Gracie giggled as they crossed over to where the race cars awaited their next adventure.

Two hours later, they occupied a booth tucked into a corner of the castle—one marked with Gracie's name. All her meals would be served at this particular table, one of the countless careful precautions that made Robyn's Place unique.

"Can we go see Fairyland next?" Gracie's eager voice pulled him from his thoughts.

"I'm sure it's a great place," Mac said.

Jen consulted her app. "We have a half-hour, but we haven't seen the animals yet. They are supposed to have penguins."

"Penguins?" Gracie gasped, launching herself from her seat before either adult could react. She darted ahead, her excitement overriding caution.

"Oh no, her shoelace!" Jen's warning came too late.

Gracie took a tumble.

McKay reached her first, finding her clutching her bleeding elbow through tears.

A crew member materialized instantly. "The infirmary is just this way. I'll show you."

McKay scooped Gracie up, noting the efficiency of the staff's response even as he hurried after their guide. The way everything operated with such precise coordination spoke of careful planning. If only his mother could be here.

Out of the corner of his eye, he saw a woman who looked so much like Dana that he nearly dropped his niece. Impossible. He refocused on getting Gracie help.

"Oh, that's cold. Why does everything that's supposed to be good for you have to hurt?" Dana winced as Chris placed a cold pack from the cooler on her ankle. How stupid had she been to walk into the gate. But that man carrying the little girl looked so much like McKay. It was her imagination. She'd seen the daily guest list. There wasn't a family surnamed Worth. McKay couldn't be here. If he was, she would have traded with someone else on the team.

Chris interrupted her thoughts. "The ice doesn't hurt."

"Bet?"

"Your nerves are extra sensitive because of the damage you did." Having completed his Advanced EMT training last week, Chris was ready to dispense his newly acquired knowledge. "You're lucky I happened to be on shift today."

Dana rolled her eyes. "It feels like we just did this."

"That was last month on a soccer field. Completely different."

"Aren't you going to get that golfer?" asked Peter. His three-year-old voice still held the adorable toddler lisp that made even his grumpiest moments endearing.

"Not golfer, gopher, st——" Porter stopped the word he was going to call his youngest sibling mid-syllable. Dana may not be able to chase anything down at the moment, but she'd mastered the look that told any child they were venturing into dangerous territory. The seven-year-old quickly changed his statement. "St—- Um, I mean, gopher and golfer do sound the same."

"A gopher hole is made by an animal, not a person playing golf." As always, the middle child and self-appointed expert on all things, Polly, was quick to offer an explanation to her younger brother.

Peter crossed his arms and glared at Chris. "So, are you going to get the gopher?"

"It wasn't a gopher hole this time that tripped up Dana." Chris locked eyes with her. "Was it Dana?"

"No gophers this time. Just me not watching where I was walking." Dana barely heard the children's banter. Her mind kept replaying the moment she'd stumbled—not because of any hole or loose shoelace, but because she'd seen a man who looked exactly like McKay. A distraction she couldn't afford on the job.

Chris took out his phone. "I'll call for a replacement and get you over to the infirmary."

"I don't need to go." That is where the man had gone.

"Mama says you should go to the doctor when you are hurt." Polly's glare left little to discuss.

A moment later, backup arrived in the form of Candace, Colin, and their security team.

"Is that the same ankle?" asked Candace.

"Yes, unfortunately." Dana winced out a smile. "It isn't as bad as last time. I am not making a habit of it."

"It was good timing. I promised the children some time away from Robyn's Place for the rest of the day. You're off duty for the rest of the day."

"If she doesn't get better quickly, can we make her ice cream again?" Peter's question was likely prompted by whatever Porter whispered in his ear.

Dana looked at Candace, who was trying not to laugh. Colin scratched his chin. "I don't know if that will help. We will have to see."

"Awe," groaned Porter.

Polly rolled her eyes. "Don't pout, Daddy means yes."

Chris helped Dana into a wheelchair he'd pulled out of some hidden corner. "Let's get that looked at."

"I feel so stupid. I did not want to be the first one to test out the infirmary."

"You're not. A guest was injured about fifteen minutes ago."

The man and the girl she saw. "How do you know that?"

"That was the text you got when you decided to go all distracted and trip over your own shoelace." Chris chuckled.

"Not that funny." Dana hit the button to open the infirmary door. "And I walked into a gate. My shoelaces are perfectly tied."

Inside, a little girl dressed in a pink princess dress held her mother's hand while she showed her father her new pink bandage. "See Uncle Mac. It's just a boo-boo."

Not her father.

Dana's heart stuttered to a stop, then started racing double-time. Of all the infirmaries in all the theme parks in all of Indiana… Dana only had a moment to collect herself before McKay turned around. Her breath caught in her throat and her heart raced. Did they have a defibrillator in here?

He spoke first. "Hi."

"Oh, poor lady! Don't worry, they're really nice here. And they have bandages in all the colors—see, I got pink!" Gracie—it had to be Gracie—thrust her elbow forward for inspection.

Dana found her voice. "It is a very nice color."

Gracie tugged on her mom's hand. "Come on, we'll miss all the fun!"

McKay didn't move to follow his sister and niece.

"Uncle Mac!"

His eyes didn't move from Dana's. "Uncle Mac will join us in a moment. He needs to talk with someone."

"Who Mommy?"

The door shut, muffling Jen's response.

Chris cleared his throat. "I'm needed elsewhere. I trust you can take this from here."

Traitor. He didn't even try to hide his knowing smile as he left.

Dana summoned the courage to look McKay in the eye. "This isn't what it looks like."

"You mean you haven't injured your ankle?"

"Well yes, but not like last time…"

His eyes swept over her and stopped on her name badge. "Do you work here?"

"Sometimes."

McKay stepped out of the way. "Do you need any help?"

Her ice pack slipped to the floor. They both reached for it, hands colliding—hot and cold all at once. He made sure she had a grip on the bag before letting go, but the brief contact left her skin tingling.

"It seems like we've done this before." His eyes searched hers.

Tears having nothing to do with her twisted ankle welled up, clogging her throat. Words wouldn't come. She looked down, struggling for composure.

McKay made a strangled sound before muttering, "Have a good day."

She tried to turn the wheelchair to follow him, but the ice pack got caught in the wheel and a nurse walked up at the same time.

"Here, let me help you."

Before Dana could protest, she was wheeled into an exam room. Could the doctor on call heal a broken heart?

Putting on a happy face should have been easier. McKay hurried to catch up with Jen and Gracie at the fairy ride. Jen raised a brow when he met them in line, but didn't comment. Like other rides, McKay ended up in a seat by himself.

Based on a story of a little fairy who found a handsome prince, this ride had more hearts and flowers than anything should.

Love.

Ha.

Dana couldn't even talk with him.

What had he thought? That she would jump out of that chair and greet him?

She had to be the clumsiest bodyguard alive.

Whoa, Mac that is uncharitable, even for you.

She worked here. She had to know that he was here. Even the custodian had greeted Gracie by name.

The end of the ride neared. McKay took a deep breath. Nothing would ruin Gracie's big day. Not even Dana Knight.

The ride ended.

"I want to ride that one again."

"I'll request that for tomorrow," said Jen.

"What is next?" asked Gracie.

Jen read her phone app. "Looks like you have a snack break."

McKay was relieved to go back to the table. He wasn't likely to run into Dana there. Could he take the coward's way out and go back to his room?

Gracie chose an oatmeal cookie and carrots for her snack. Jen did the same. The server didn't leave. Jen kicked McKay's foot.

"Oh, sorry, nothing for me."

"But Uncle Mac. These snacks are healthy. You should eat."

McKay looked at the server and ordered a glass of water.

Gracie huffed. Their food arrived only a minute later, distracting Gracie with a cookie.

Jen's concerned mother look turned on McKay full force. "I think someone needs to have a timeout and find his happy place."

Gracie crossed her arms. "You can't give Uncle Mac a time out."

"Oh yes, I can. I think twenty minutes should be long enough." Jen snapped off a bite of her carrot.

"That is a very long time," said Gracie.

"He can stay here while we go to the Mermaid Pond."

Twenty minutes to collect himself. "Maybe I should write out lines too. Do you have any paper?"

Jen dug through her little bag, which had to come from a Mary Poppins store, and produced a pen and a small notebook. "Here you go. Write: 'I will not be a bore,' 100 times."

Twenty-four

THE DOCTOR LEFT THE ROOM to get a walking boot. Dana sent off a hurried text.

DANA: He is here. What do I do?

BRIT: Run after him!

DANA: I just injured my ankle.

SIMONE: Again?

BRIT: Then hobble after him. *laughing*

DANA: I can't.

SIMONE: That was what you said about the email you deleted.

Not deleted exactly. Hidden deep in drafts.

BRIT: This is your running through Bath moment. If you don't find him, you will sit in coach on every flight for the rest of your life!

The doctor entered to find Dana laughing. "You're sure you don't want something for your pain? Laughter can be a body's coping response to pain."

"No, it's just my friend being funny."

"Here is your boot. Stay off of it as much as you can today. Ice. If it doesn't feel better in three days, come back."

Dana thanked him and signed the necessary papers. She stepped out of the infirmary. Where could McKay be?

Since she wasn't technically employed by Robyn's Place, she didn't have access to the security side of the guest app. Chris would. Maybe he would give her a clue.

She spotted Gracie and Jen before she found Chris.

"Hi Gracie!" Dana followed protocol and talked to the guest of honor first. "How is your elbow?"

The little girl looked at her arm. "Fine."

"Glad to hear the pink bandage is doing its job." There was no sign of McKay.

Gracie looked at Dana's black boot and wrinkled her nose. "They didn't make that very pretty."

"They save the pretty stuff for the guests." Dana looked around again. "Is your uncle still here?"

"Mommy put him in timeout." Gracie giggled. "He has to write that he won't be boring."

Jen's lips thinned.

"Jen. I know I'm probably the reason for him needing a time out. Will you tell me where he is?"

"We left him in the Castle."

"Gracie, —" Jen held out the last syllable long enough for Gracie to realize she'd misspoke. "He is in the castle at our table."

"Thank you." Dana turned.

"Miss Knight. I hope you have a code of honor that doesn't include breaking hearts."

"I hope I am off to a rescue and not to fight a dragon."

Gracie giggled. "You two are funny."

Dana smiled. "We are just making jokes because my last name is Knight. Like the ones who used to rescue princesses."

"Oh, go on then." Gracie waved her off.

Dana hobbled to the castle. This would be easier if she had a mighty steed. *This isn't the Royal Crescent, but it should do.*

McKay crumpled up another piece of paper. He didn't have the words. Part of him wanted to tell Dana exactly how he felt—hurt, love, and all. The other part of him wanted to tell her, "Thank you, but it's over." Unfortunately, his heart refused to believe his brain on the latter.

He needed a plan. If he found that other bodyguard who had been with Dana, maybe he could find out how to contact her. They needed to have this out once and for all.

A conversation at the door to the private dining room caught his attention.

"Miss, you can't go in there. Miss, you are not cleared, employee or not."

Dana's voice stopped his heart. "I am aware of that. Will you please tell Mr. Worth I would like to talk to him?"

Dana had found him. His feet carried him across the floor before his mind could protest.

"I'm sorry, sir," said the server. "You understand I can't let anyone but your family into this room."

"Yes, thank you."

McKay stepped out into the corridor. The server continued to stand there. Dana looked at him, then at the server.

"I promise I will not step in. I just need to have a private conversation with Mr. Worth."

The server said something McKay didn't quite catch before he turned and left.

McKay stepped closer. Apparently, his feet were in line with his heart. "How is your—"

Dana put up a hand. "Please, McKay. I'm so sorry. I'm so, so sorry."

McKay wasn't sure if he was more shocked at the apology or the tear that rolled down Dana's cheek.

"You don't have to—"

She held up her hand to stop him. "Please. Please let me get through this. I'm sorry I didn't talk to you on the plane. I'm sorry I didn't give you a chance. I'm sorry I didn't send all the emails I've written."

"You wrote me emails?"

"Please. I need to—" She took a deep breath before speaking. "I'm sorry I couldn't talk coherently in the infirmary. I was so shocked."

The tears started in earnest now.

McKay pulled her into a hug. "I'm sorry about not telling you about the sting on the ship. I'm sorry for not giving you the Claddagh ring on the Cobb."

"Wait? What?" She pulled back just far enough to look at him.

"I went back and bought the rose gold ring you liked. I nearly gave it to you on the Cobb. It was in my pocket. I wasn't sure if I should."

Instead of her tears stopping, they flowed in earnest soaking his shirt.

"Look, Mommy! Uncle Mac got out of timeout without permission. Does that mean he isn't boring anymore?"

All the adults laughed. Gracie joined them with a confused look on her face.

"You're right Gracie. I left without permission." McKay kept one arm around Dana.

"It looks like I need to send him to his room." Jen said through her laughter.

Dana stepped back and wiped her eyes.

"If the Knight is crying, does that mean she lost?" asked Gracie.

McKay had no idea what his niece meant.

Jen and Dana laughed. Again.

Dana squatted down as much as the boot would let her. "No Gracie, I am pretty sure I didn't lose. But I need to talk to your uncle for a while to be sure."

"But Mommy said he had to go to his room."

Mac took Dana's hand. "I think it would be preferable if she just sent me outside instead."

Jen covered her laugh. "Yes, yes. Outside is best and don't come back until you've kissed and made up."

McKay pulled Dana closer. "That is what I intend to do."

Epilogue

Izzy stood beside the wedding photographer, phone ready to capture the moment she'd been invited to film. Her parents beamed from their seats, as proud of their daughter's role in this romance as if they'd match made it themselves.

Dana slipped her arm through her father's. "Are you ready for this?"

"The question is, are you ready?" His eyes glistened with pride and perhaps a few tears.

They followed Cheyanne, resplendent in the sage green bridesmaid dress Dana had planned to wear just weeks ago. Her sister had insisted on wearing it, saying it brought their story full circle. Despite the rushed wedding plans, the church overflowed with loved ones. Brit and Simone sat with Javier, Chris, and Tian, all of them grinning like they'd personally orchestrated this ending. Well, they did have a hand in it. ZoElle and Alan were absent, their new baby was not up to traveling yet. The Ogilvie children clustered near the front with Gracie, their flower-petal warfare having left a colorful battlefield in their wake.

McKay's mother sat in the front row; her smile radiant despite her obvious fatigue. The rushed wedding was worth having her in attendance. Dana hoped to get to know her better in the next few weeks, so that in the coming years she could pass on stories about Grandma Worth to grandchildren whom her new mother-in-law would never meet.

Even Sheila was there, seated alone, but looking happy. Their tentative new understanding holding for this day, at least. Though given the opportunity, Sheila declined joining Dad in walking Dana down the aisle, claiming she'd done so little to raise Dana that it didn't seem right. However Sheila even paid for Dana's wedding dress, a shock that still had Dana smiling. They shared a glance full of forgiveness—not for everything, but enough to begin healing.

Following the time-honored tradition, her father placed Dana's hand in McKay's. As the minister spoke, the words seemed both endless and fleeting. Dana barely heard them, lost in memories of the Cobb, of midnight walks in Bath, of all the moments that had led them here.

McKay slid the diamond and emerald ring on her finger, replacing the Claddagh ring she'd worn throughout their three-week-long engagement and would continue to wear at work. An Irish honeymoon, complete with castle visits, would wait until next spring, a gift from McKay's mother, who told them both she didn't want them grieving for long.

When the minister finally pronounced them man and wife, McKay's thumb brushed her cheek with infinite tenderness before his lips found hers, sealing their vows to the cheers of their friends and the delighted giggles of the children.

In the back of the church, Izzy cheered the loudest. Her video would perfectly tell the story—from that first impulsive kiss on the Cobb to this carefully planned one, proving that sometimes the best love stories aren't found in Jane Austen novels, but in real life.

Note

I'D NEVER HEARD OF THE Blood Donation Hall of Fame until my friend and longtime proof editor was inducted as I was writing the first draft of this story. Nanette's selfless acts of donating ten gallons of whole blood (and counting) and many, many hours working at blood drives is a great example to all. To honor her, I had to sneak in this information someplace, even if I didn't find a way to make the character more like her. (Although she is a wise and loving parent, like Dana's father.) To the best of my knowledge, the facts I snuck in are correct.

Twenty-five years ago, I needed to receive blood during an emergency surgery. The rural hospital I was in struggled to deal with the situation given their resources. I am unclear if that included blood, however I know that despite loosing nearly half the blood in my body, I didn't receive any. (Obviously, prayers were answered and I lived.)

As always, there is a need for blood donations. I urge those of my readers who can, to donate regularly. Please contact your local donation centers for more information.

To learn more about the National Blood Donation Hall of Fame https://www.fresenius-kabi.com/us/news-and-events/fresenius-kabi-celebrates-25th-anniversary-of-national-blood-don

Acknowledgements

Some of you know that this one has been an especially long time coming as it is a year late. A huge thanks to Tammy who helped me put this book on hold so it didn't sink.

Thanks to Nanette, who is so willing to help make all my projects better. I would never make it through a day without Maria and Cindy, whose texts and messages keep me writing. Special thanks to Mara who kept hoping this one would come. Big thanks to Julie for the excellent edits. Thank you!

A special thanks to E.B. Wheeler, who planned the best Janeite tour of England ever Much of my inspiration comes from that trip. My husband deserves special thanks for arranging our Irish cruise and supporting me while I used a knee scooter. He literally had to drag me up some hills.

My family, for sharing their home with the fictional characters who often get fed better than they do. Seriously, I haven't cooked in years.

And to my Father in Heaven for putting these wonderful people, and any I may have forgotten to mention, in my life. I am grateful for every experience and blessing I have been granted.

About the Author

LORIN GRACE WAS BORN IN Colorado and has been moving around the country ever since, living in eight states and several imaginary worlds. She holds a degree in graphic design which comes in handy with creating book covers. Currently, she lives with her husband, and a dog who is insanely jealous of her laptop.

When not writing, Lorin enjoys creating graphics, visiting historical sites, museums, painting furniture, and reading. Three of her books, her debut novel, *Waking Lucy* (2017), *Mending Fences* (2018), and *Not the Bodyguard's Baby* (2020) have won Recommend Read awards in the League of Utah Writers Published book contest.

She loves to here from her readers at lg@loringrace.com

To learn more or follow her newsletter at LorinGrace.com

www.ingramcontent.com/pod-product-compliance
Lightning Source LLC
Chambersburg PA
CBHW060358310726
48976CB00003B/873